# WRITE AGAIN:
## A collection of stories, articles memoirs, and poems

### By 29 Wichita area authors

All proceeds of this book go to
Senior Services Inc. of Wichita, KS
A not-for-profit charity.

## Starla Criser

# 2018 © Starla Enterprises, Inc.

All rights reserved. No part of this publication may be reproduced, stored in a retrieval system, or transmitted in any form or by any means without prior written permission of the publisher or by the individual authors, except by a reviewer who may quote brief passages in a review to be printed in a newspaper, magazine or journal. Individual authors retain copyright for their work.

For information regarding permission, write to Starla Enterprises, Inc.
Attention: Permissions Department,
9415 E. Harry St., Ste. 603, Wichita, KS 67207

First Edition

ISBN: 978-0-578-40977-1

Editor & Cover Design by Starla Criser

Printed in the U.S.A.

Write Again: A collection of stories, articles, memoirs, and poems

## TABLE OF CONTENTS

| TITLE | AUTHOR |
|---|---|
| Being Old Is A State of Mind | Coe Holden |
| A Sister's Letter | Rochelle Boster |
| Philosophical Knowtions | Sherry A. Phillips |
| Friendship | Bonnie Creekmore |
| Forever Wrapped Around My Heart | Starla Criser |
| Haiku for Boomers | Connie Holt |
| My "Fix-It" Daddy | Jan Koelsch |
| Miz Rita, The Palmist | Gwendolyn Eldridge Gandy |
| How Lovely is the Quiet | Martha Williams Prentice |
| Lessons from Stubby | Jan Koelsch |
| Memories of Joyland | Debbi McGinn Elmore |
| A Creamy Crescent Moon | Martha Williams Prentice |
| Unlikely Discovery | Beverly J. Hamilton |
| My First Airplane Ride | Bonnie Lacey Krenning |
| Thought for the Day | Tom Elman |
| Boldea's Laws | Don Boldea |
| A Storm and Granddad's House Remembered | Beverly J. Hamilton |
| Garden Time | Sherry A. Phillips |
| James | Caroline Grace |
| The Hidden House | E. L. Morrow |
| Hiking Across Kansas | Rowena Hinshaw |
| Petty Poi | Herbert Ingram |
| Life on Mars | Susan Howell |
| Farm Memories | Debbi McGinn Elmore |

## Starla Criser

| | |
|---|---|
| Our Daddy's Righteous Anger | Sharon Revell |
| Celebrating Kansas City Royals 50th Anniversary | Maudyne Cline |
| There I Stood | Don Boldea |
| The Mulberry Tree | Bonnie Lacey Krenning |
| Kansas Wheat Harvest Evolved Through the Decades | Debbi McGinn Elmore |
| A Butterfly Landed Suddenly | Martha Williams Prentice |
| Lola | Bunnie Clark |
| An Unfinished Story | Lola |
| I Was Walking Barefoot | Donita M. Davis |
| The Love of a Child | Ann Alvis |
| It's Not All About the Outside | Starla Criser |
| The Master Chef | Bonnie Creekmore |
| Good Morning | Don Boldea |
| Carnival Summer Camp | Theresa L. Reiter |
| Forever Home | Jan Koelsch |
| There You Stood Upon the Bridge | Martha Williams Prentice |
| Your Eyes & On the Stage | Coe Holden |
| My Three Pets | E. L. Morrow |
| Harry's Date | Gwendolyn Eldridge Gandy |
| Doctor Trip | Susan Howell |
| The Dust Bowl in Kansas | Mabel Helen Braddy (via Joan Morrison) |
| Fall Colors | Joan E. Morrison |
| Venus Rising High, So High | Martha Williams Prentice |
| Who We Are! | Rochelle Boster |
| Living | Bonnie Lacey Krenning |
| The Spur Ranch Deer | Caroline Grace |
| Humble Pie | R. E. Brown |
| Trip Down the Alaska Canada Highway | Joan E. Morrison |
| The Poet | Coe Holden |

# Write Again: A collection of stories, articles, memoirs, and poems

| | |
|---|---|
| Memories | Maudyne Cline |
| The Photo Album | Jan Koelsch |
| The Gift | Donita M. Davis |
| Code 3 Revisited | Lois Ann Seiwert |
| I Have Fallen and I Can't Get Up | Beverly J. Hamilton |
| Book Club Ladies | Gwendolyn Eldridge Gandy |
| If We See You | Sharon Lee Brown |
| At Workday's End | Bonnie Creekmore |
| The Other Half of Me | Beverly J. Hamilton |
| I Went Out to Look at the Sky | Martha Williams Prentice |
| Talkin' Proper | Bonnie Lacey Krenning |
| The Hay Hook Killer of White Oak Mountain | Gerald McCoy |
| The Next Journey, Retirement | Rochelle Boster |
| Listen, I Heard a Bird This Hour | Martha Williams Prentice |
| Winner | Starla Criser |
| To Town at Christmastime | Bonnie Lacey Krenning |
| My Wichita | Don Boldea |
| I Saw a Hawk in the Morning Sky | Martha Williams Prentice |
| Mama's Kitchen | Rochelle Boster |
| Medicine Man | Bonnie Creekmore |
| My Christmas Trees | Bonnie Lacey Krenning |
| The Toy | Coe Holden |
| Sometimes I See a Simple Thing | Martha Williams Prentice |
| Conundrum | Rochelle Boster |
| White Christmas | Bonnie Lacey Krenning |
| A Dragonfly from a Nearby Glade | Martha Williams Prentice |
| The Christmas Cabin | Ann Alvis |

## LIST OF CONTRIBUTORS
### And Entry Locations

| AUTHOR | PAGE LOCATIONS |
|---|---|
| Alvis, Ann | 82-84, 204-220 |
| Boldea, Don | 35, 59, 90, 187-188 |
| Boster, Rochelle | 9-10, 123-124, 179-180, 187-188, 190-192, 198-199 |
| Brown, R. E. | 135-136 |
| Brown, Sharon Lee | 166-167 |
| Clark, Bunnie | 70-75, 76-80 |
| Cline, Maudyne | 58, 143-144 |
| Creekmore, Bonnie | 12, 88-89, 162-163, 193 |
| Criser, Starla | 13-14, 85-87, 182 |
| Davis, Donita M. | 81, 148-149 |
| Elman, Tom | 33-34 |
| Elmore, Debbi McGinn | 24-27, 51-55, 63-66 |
| Gandy, Gwendolyn Eldridge | 19-20, 111-112, 159-161 |
| Grace, Caroline | 41, 133-134 |

## Write Again: A collection of stories, articles, memoirs, and poems

| | |
|---|---|
| Hamilton, Beverly J. | 29-30, 36-39, 157-158, 164 |
| Hinshaw, Rowena | 47-48 |
| Holden, Coe | 8, 98, 142, 196 |
| Holt, Connie | 15-16 |
| Howell, Susan | 50, 113-114 |
| Ingram, Herbert | 49 |
| Koelsch, Jan | 17-18, 22-23, 94-96, 145-147 |
| Krenning, Bonnie Lacey | 31-31, 60-62, 125-132, 168-169, 183-186, 194-195, 200-202 |
| McCoy, Gerald | 170-178 |
| Morrison, Joan E. | 115-116, 117-121, 137-141 |
| Morrow, E. L. | 42-46, 99-110 |
| Phillips, Sherry A. | 11, 40 |
| Prentice, Martha Williams | 21, 28, 67-69, 97, 122, 165, 181, 189, 197, 203 |
| Reiter, Theresa L. | 91-93 |
| Revell, Sharon | 56-57 |
| Seiwert, Lois Ann | 150-156 |

## BEING OLD IS A STATE OF MIND
### Coe Holden

Being old so I have been told is just a state of mind

You have to leave your worries behind

Worries will make you wrinkled and gray

You don't want to look this way

So chin up and put a smile on your face

And if you can, pick up the pace.

If getting old is just a state of mind

My hair and looks I have left behind somewhere in the past

But as I look back, life has been a blast.

## A SISTER'S LETTER

Rochelle Boster

October 7, 2008

To Whom It May Concern:

Ninety days. You told me it would take ninety days for my sister to adjust to her new surroundings and to settle into her new way of life. Ninety days to adjust to a lack of freedom. She could no longer drive or enjoy her favorite chocolate malts from Braums. She could not walk around the lake in the park.

She needed ninety days to settle into a new church. And to mourn the loss of her circle of friends and the safety in the sanctuary she understood.

Thank you for reassuring me ninety days would heal her homesickness and ease her paranoia. Paranoia so strong that she hides everything of value to her. Sometimes under the bed, in the pages of books, or in cereal boxes in kitchen cabinets. My sister braces the door with a chair because she is sure someone has a key to her apartment.

For a woman who doesn't understand much anymore ninety days is a long time in her life. She can't remember when or what she has eaten. She can't recall who came to see her or when she last talked to her children.

Thank you for telling me the medicine she is taking for the ninety days will slow the progress of the disease. A disease stealing her memories of all she has held precious in her life. Medicine she can't remember to take.

Thank you for letting me know that in ninety days, only 129,600 minutes, my sister would have a new routine, new friends and new activities to keep her busy.

Let me share with you what my sister has at the end of ninety days. She has a new key to her front door because she insisted the old lock had to be changed. She has chronic diarrhea from eating food she finds too spicy in the dining room. She has acquaintances, not friends, that she eats with each day and then meets anew the next. She carries anger and frustration and expresses it by crying and cursing. My sister has $2,500.00 in traveler's checks hidden somewhere in her apartment, because she wants to run away from her new home.

I wish you had told me that there is no definitive end to the changes my sister will experience. They will only escalate until she is a totally changed person. The truth would have been easier to understand and accept as it unfolded. My sister's ninety days will start over and over again, as will mine. This will repeat until there is nothing left of her and her journey is complete.

Sincerely,

Broken Hearted

## PHILOSOPHICAL KNOWTIONS

Sherry A. Phillips

Things we didn't know we had to know
- Our blood type
- How to set a clock
- Value of flossing your teeth
- How to choose an energy-saving light bulb
- How to avoid clichés

Things we hope they don't find out we found out
- The stash of pornographic cartoons hidden on the top shelf in my parent's bedroom
- Grandad Swinger ate soda crackers with milk and sugar without his teeth
- Grandfather Hager was alive when we were always told he was dead
- My nephew's eyelid was torn by a brassier strap hook
- What happens when you drink a blender full of Margaritas

Untraceable
- My mother's second husband
- How my Grandfather Hager got on the Dunlap School Board
- Amelia Earhardt's plane crash
- Who invented thumbsucking
- The source of ear wax

## FRIENDSHIP

Bonnie Creekmore

Friendship is a special thing

Not bound by age or reason.

It matters not what color skin

Or wealth or fame or season.

It is a gift from God above

For anyone to claim

Who will share His gift of love

For others, in His name.

We have that special gift, you know

We laugh and talk and share

Our gladness and our sorrow

Knowing there's someone to care.

So have a Happy Birthday, Friend,

Make memories that sing

And give you hope for future days

With the joys they bring.

## FOREVER WRAPPED AROUND MY HEART

### Starla Criser

The first time I held my daughter's hand was beyond amazing. This small human being was a precious gift to us, someone who would forever be a part of our lives.

Her hand was so tiny, not even as big as one of my fingers. So soft, so fragile, pudgy too. How could it wrap around my heart? How could it have me or my husband wrapped around it?

There is no logic to any of that. The bonding just happens. Not to every parent. But it happened to us.

My beloved daughter had my heart from her first cry. Okay, middle of the night crying for some unknown reason tested that. Not much, though. You tune those moments out. They don't matter. This tiny person belonging to you is all that matters… and you belonging to that small person.

She and I held hands for so many reasons. Parental guidance for safety as we crossed a parking lot or a street. Fun times when she held both my hand and her dad's as we lifted her up and she swung between us, giggling. Sad times in comfort at too many funerals.

We rarely hold hands anymore, which saddens me now that I think about it. Instead, we touch each other's lives in different ways. We talk by phone almost every day, sharing our lives. Or we text to share a quick thought. Sometimes we send a photo or a web link, or many other things.

When we're together, often she and I will sit beside each other. Often snuggled close. Sometimes I tickle her, always she complains about that. Age doesn't matter.

She will always be my daughter, a part of me. These days she is more than that. She is one of my best friends, someone I can confide in, someone she can confide in. We can share life's trials. We can laugh and cry together. Hearing her laugh or seeing her beautiful smile fills me with such amazing love.

Love that started when I first held her in my arms. Love that began when I first touched that delicate little hand.

## HAIKU FOR BOOMERS

Connie Holt

My only regret

Is that I have no regrets

What a boring life!

Dark and swollen clouds

Stifling calm before the storm

Darn—no umbrella!

Once Urban Cowboys

Now, some golf playing grandpas

A cart is their steed.

The older I get

The faster my watch doth run

Time rockets by me.

I have no green thumb

My touch is the kiss of death

To the poor flora.

We love Rock and Roll
Though the juke boxes have fled,
We keep on dancin'!

"It's smothering here!"
"No, it feels comfortable."
A she said he said.

Where should we eat out?
"Mexican?" "Let's do Chinese."
Why did he ask me?

My needs are simple—
Coffee and my newspaper
Heaven in a chair!

My famous last words:
"My age is just a number."
My number's 'bout up!

## MY "FIX-IT" DADDY

Jan Koelsch

God,

He has always been the "fix-it" Daddy.

> I could take anything to Dad as a child. He could fix it.
>
> Dad could fix anything for me as a teenager.
>
> As a young adult, I could take the problems to Dad. He would fix them.

Now my fix-it Daddy needs Someone to fix him.

God,

> He is sick and needs Your healing touch.
>
> Please be the Great Physician. Please fix all that is wrong with my Daddy.
>
> I place my Dad in Your hands.

Thank you for all the time we have had with him.

Thank you for a man who never fails us and always is there for us.

Thank you for keeping him safe.

Please, O God, keep my Mom close. Please touch her with Your healing hand.

I love you, God. May Your will be done. [I hope that will mean healing my parents].

God,

> My fix-it Daddy fought long and hard.

He looked to You for strength in the most difficult battle of his life.

He knew You were with him in that battle, too.

He also knew that a call from You meant rest and permanent healing.

So on August 9, 1999, he answered Your call and went home.

He was ready to go home to You,

I know that was the best thing for him.

I just wanted him to stay as long as possible.

Thank You, God, for letting my fix-it Daddy be with us as long as You did.

Most of all, God, thank You for fixing my Daddy

Forever.

You see, God, if there is anything that You need fixed in heaven---

A gate hinge, a jewel put back in place, something on the roof of a mansion,

Whatever may need repaired,

My Fix-it Daddy can and will fix-it for You.

We will miss him. I know You and he will be watching out for us.

Thank you.


In Your Son's name,

Jan*

*The first part of this writing was written when my dad was diagnosed with lung cancer. The second part of this writing was written on August 9, 1999 on the day he died. He lived 18 months after his diagnosis.

## MIZ RITA, THE PALMIST

Gwendolyn Eldridge Gandy

It was a gray cold rainy day outside, and the clouds appeared to cover every inch of the sky. This is the sort of cozy time you would rather stay in bed or just sit in a comfortable chair with a cup of hot tea and a really good mystery book. Well, that won't be happening for me today, because I had promised my best friend Judy that I'd go with her to meet Miz Rita the fortune teller.

Judy had read an advertisement in our local newspaper about Miz Rita. The article supposedly told how she could assist people with their problems or to find their wealth, happiness and love. Judy is sure Rita will give her the tools for the life changing help she needs and wants. I must have been crazy when I agreed to go along with her to this meeting. It's not only frightening and funny at the same time, but it's downright stupid. You never know what they might tell you. I wish I hadn't agreed to go.

*\*\*\*\*\**

Miz Rita answered the doorbell on the first ring. She rushed us into a dimly lit room, with one small window, and decorated with used furniture and ornaments. She had a on a long navy-blue dress that looked like a nightgown. Her make-up was quite unique. Her snow-white face powder was almost frightening along with black lipstick. She had polished eyebrows and fingernails so long they curled under at the tips. Miz Rita's dyed red hair was sticking-up straight on her head. It looked like a perm-gone-wrong, or she had just pulled her finger out of the wall socket. I can say her picture in the newspaper didn't do her justice.

I am sure she must have been a stage actress at one time. Where else would she have learned how to put on that type of make-up and get away with wearing that theatrical look. Life is a stage and we all want to do our best and look our best. Miz Rita brings a feeling of calmness and a smile to our faces. Judy and Rita really got along well with each other in the time they had spent together. It was exciting and informative for Judy.

Sitting and listening to them talking and laughing made me realize how magical this time was for both. Judy got answers to her questions and things to work on in her life, and she made a new friend. It was all well worth the price, whatever it was.

## HOW LOVELY IS THE QUIET
### Martha Williams Prentice

How lovely is the quiet of
    this early morning hour
when I alone am witnessing
    the bloom of Glory's flower,
which glistens under drops of dew
    that fell from sacred font
to take my breath a moment,
    then, my heart forever haunt.

# LESSONS FROM STUBBY

## Jan Koelsch

Stubby was our 15-year-old miniature Schnauzer. He was black and silver and stood about 14 inches from his withers to the floor. Stubby was such a sweet, gentle spirit with that terrier mentality. He was named Stubby because of his short tail. Actually, I think Stubby was short for stubborn. Stubby passed October 12, 2017. At a routine vet visit the vet found he had a malignant melanoma in his mouth, stage IV bladder and lung cancer. We felt with the pain he was in, the kindest thing we could do for him was to let him go the dog heaven, also known as the Rainbow Bridge. As you know when you have a Schnauzer in your life, you live in their world. So I paid attention to the things he taught me. Not having Stubby physically with us is hard. Our routine is different. Life is different. We miss him and always will. We also have his paw prints all over our hearts.

*Things I Learned from Stubby*

1. We should be nice and friendly to each other.
2. Spend some time outside every day. The sun is good for you. You won't melt if it is raining.
3. Take time to play.
4. Meet people with a smile. They will smile back.
5. Listening is better than talking. No one listens to each other anymore.
6. Always meet your new neighbors.
7. Talking at the fence with your neighbors is good.
8. Riding in the car with your family is great.

9. Walks around the park are good for you.
10. It doesn't pay to stay angry or carry a grudge.
11. If you bark long enough, someone will come to see what is going on.
12. Be fierce no matter how big or small you are.
13. Be curious. You never know what you will find.
14. Be alert and be prepared.
15. Always have one person in your life that you can count on and who is on your side.
16. People need unconditional love and so do dogs and other animals, like squirrels.
17. When you get old, each day is a new day.
18. Be patient with others. They may not be having a good day.
19. Pain may be part of your life but the attitude you have can make it better.
20. Be forgiving if someone hurts you (like the vet). Most of the time it was not intentional.
21. Get excited sometimes.
22. Have fun.
23. Love unconditionally.
24. Be there for those you love and they will be there for you.
25. Treats are good anytime.
26. Waiting is part of life.

# MEMORIES OF JOYLAND

Debbi McGinn Elmore

As a boy growing up in south Wichita, Patrick Flanigan spent nearly every waking hour at Joyland Amusement Park, swimming, riding the rides, and honing his pitching and shooting skills.

"I practically lived in the swimming pool," he says with a laugh. "I was fascinated with the clown. The first thing I would do is run up to make sure he was playing the organ properly."

He was also enamored by the go-cart racing and waited impatiently to get old enough to drive. The path to the go-carts led past the picnic area, and he says he remembers families bringing picnic lunches and enjoying the area. Many company picnics were held there as well, and the owners of Joyland never objected to outside vendors catering those events.

"My dad played pro baseball, and we were catching and throwing baseballs ever since I was little," he recalls. "So, I got very good at winning the prizes. As a teenager, I used to take my dates to Joyland, and they would always go home with a large stuffed animal. It was a great place to go because it was safe."

"I have two favorite memories of Joyland," Gina Barker reminisces. "Fun night for school was so fun. Our parents would drop us off and we would run from ride to ride. I felt so free. My favorite was the roller coaster; that's when my love for roller coasters began. The other was KFDI Day. It was really crowded. I loved the crowds; everyone had a great time. We would eat in the park which was to me the coolest thing ever. It was a special treat to go there. Many of my favorite childhood memories were at Joyland."

Doug Stark's reaction to the roller coaster was the complete opposite. "I am absolutely not a roller coaster guy, so the few times I did it I hated it," he says, noting the Tilt-a-Whirl and the Spider were okay, but he was fine when the rides were over.

"As I grew up in a family where my grandparents supplied most of the concessions that existed in the area, whether Joyland Amusement Park or most high schools, WSU, etc., although probably weird, I was always interested in what they were selling and what volume they were doing. I will say that the owners, Stan and Margaret Nelson and their son-in-law Bill Hagaman were probably the nicest and classiest people I ever dealt with when I was involved in the business during the 1980s."

Joyland was founded by Lester Ottaway and his sons Herbert and Harold in 1949. Once the largest theme park in central Kansas, it was in continuous operation for 55 years, from June 12, 1949 to 2004, closing permanently in 2006.

Margaret was in high school when she went to work at Joyland. While there, she met Stan Nelson, who was originally from New York and was working as a ticket seller. He became the office manager and he and Margaret married in 1950. They purchased the park from the Ottaways in 1973. The couple worked hard at the park while simultaneously raising their four children.

After five decades, the Nelsons sold Joyland to a young man who failed to make a go of the enterprise. They went to the city to seek support for Joyland, but there was no interest. Eventually, Joyland closed.

"It was very joyous," Margaret says of their years at Joyland. "I loved working with my husband. It was a wonderful experience and a lot of work."

During their 50 years at Joyland, they helped to create magical memories for generations. Nearly everyone over the age of 40 has a special memory.

"My strongest memory was having the crap scared out of me the first time I rode the roller coaster," says Mark Mains, noting he rode it for the first time with David Snell, now an actor in Hollywood. "I loved the Whacky Shack and bumper cars. Honestly the first thing I always did was give trash to the pig! There was one ride I never rode. Always had a line and thought I would just ride it next time. I think it was called the Zipper. Still regret not going on it!"

"I remember attending picnics for the company my father worked for," recalls Marsha Hills. "We could ride all the rides all day long.

Joyland was always a fun place to go on a date! As a young mother my memories of Joyland were with my children. In addition to going to Joyland with friends and their children, each year Joyland would have a night where their grade school could go and ride all the rides for one price and it was a fundraiser for the school PTO group.

"My husband remembers him and his friends riding their bikes to Joyland," she adds. "They would play a baseball game as long as their money would hold out. He recalls that the pinball type game cost somewhere around five or 10 cents. He remembers if they could get their hands on some additional money they would ride the bumper cars.

"It was especially fun to go to Joyland at night so that you could enjoy all the lights of the rides. I also remember vividly Louie the clown. He greeted you as you arrived. My cousin was scared to death of him and so we always had a little fun with that."

"I remember being too afraid to ride anything, but I was fascinated by watching the rides and imagining what it would be like," recalls Craig Thompson. "I got over that fear by the way, but now no one will ride with me."

He also remembers one afternoon when he and a classmate had Joyland pretty much to themselves. "We were the only ones on the bumper cars, so we made it a racetrack chasing each other around the unoccupied cars. My wife, Laura, remembers saving the Kitty Clover blue chips and grade cards for tickets. My grades would have been worth one trip down the giant slide which was Laura's favorite ride."

Saving grades for tickets is a reference to Scholarship Day, a much-anticipated event for students whose parents may not have had much money for routine visits to Joyland. On Scholarship Day, grades were redeemable for ride tickets, and the park was even more crowded than usual.

"In grade school and junior high, when we got our report cards at the end of the year, you got so many tickets for every A, B, etc.," recalls Laurel Alkire. "I was in Catholic school then and in 7th grade, both me and my friend had a huge crush on the same boy. I think she was a bit more 'lovesick' than I. I remember we were walking toward the Tilt-A-Whirl when we saw him. He asked me if I wanted to go on a ride with him. Of course I said yes! Remember, that ride would throw you from side to side, so you would be leaning in to the other person. Best Tilt-A-Whirl ride I ever went on!"

Since it closed in 2006, Joyland has been subjected to numerous incidents of vandalism and looting. Nearly every building is covered with graffiti, the administration offices have been destroyed, and many of the park's vintage items have been stolen. A grassroots effort to raise money to restore Joyland got underway but failed to raise the needed funds and was called off with the announcement in 2015 that the old amusement park, site of so many happy memories, would be razed. A sad announcement for many, tempered by Margaret's gift of the carousel to Botanica, where it will delight future generations and stand as a memorial to Joyland Amusement Park.

## A CREAMY CRESCENT MOON

Martha Williams Prentice

A creamy crescent moon
  in a navy-blue sky
    behind filigreed branches
      that sway outside the window
        framed with sheer white panels
          which flutter, now, and then
            and sweep against the edge of the bed
            by a wandering wind,

a wind that carries the tinkling tones
  of windchimes from the patio below
    back and forth, low and lulling,
      and lifts the sweet essence of honeysuckle
        from its moon-lit white blossoms
          up, up, to be inhaled
            slow and deep, with eyes closed
              to remember your kiss upon my lips.

## UNLIKELY DISCOVERY

Beverly J. Hamilton

A young Derbyite named Lucas, a metal detecting enthusiast, was scouring his property on south Derby Street when he discovered a class ring. On closer examination he saw that it had initials and dates legible. His search for its owner began.

After cleaning the ring of its dirt and grime from years of being buried underground its brilliance and definition amazed him. He took his find to the Derby High School where he asked the staff to provide him a 1958 Year Book. There he planned to match the initials on the ring to a student's name in that class. Oddly enough upon first examination of the book he noted the book's editor's initials were the same as those on the ring. Concluding his complete search of the book the outcome was the editor of the 1958 class year book was the only female with the ring's initials, BH. Lucas' search was progressing. He was sure he knew the ring's owner. The question now was where this person lived and what was her name now. Was she even still living?

One of the school staff knew a possible relative of BH, so she contacted her. She verified BH still lived in the Wichita area and identified her married name. Lucas located a phone number and made the call.

When Beverly answered the phone and heard the story, she inquired where he had found the ring. Lucas told her the location, and she volunteered that she had lived next door to that location 54 years ago, 1966-1972. She had a perennial flower bed along the fence where he had found the ring. She asked if it had a green and white stone. He indicated it did, and it seemed in perfect condition.

It thrilled both parties to bring closure to the story of the lost and found class ring. It was amazing to say at last the ring and owner met again after so many years of separation all due to new technology and old-fashioned caring by a gentleman named Lucas. Ring and owner celebrated together in the spring of 2018, sixty years after high school graduation.

## MY FIRST AIRPLANE RIDE

Bonnie Lacey Krenning

On a beautiful Sunday afternoon about a month after Bill and I met in March we were out riding in his 1931 Model A with the windows rolled down. Two of his bridge painting buddies were in the back seat. Bill was the only one who had a car, besides the boss, so the guys were often in our company. As we drove into the lovely countryside, we heard the engine noise and saw a small airplane flying low in the sky.

After watching for a while I said, "I always wanted to fly in an airplane, ever since I was a little girl and I saw my first plane flying like a bird in the sky." After a few moments Bill said, "Well, now is as good a day as any." He surprised me by turning the car around and heading toward the highway.

Down the highway there was an airport about 20 miles away that gave rides on Sunday afternoon in an open cockpit, low-wing, single-engine plane. When we arrived at the airport Bill and I got out of the car; the guys got out more slowly. They were captive passenger, I guess. The guys urged me to go first because I was a girl, pretending to be polite. I suspect they weren't as eager to fly as I was. Bill paid two dollars for my ride; a lot of money in 1947; but since Bill offered I wasn't about to not go.

As I walked with the pilot toward the plane, I noticed that he was grinning. I saw no other women or girls there. He probably didn't have many female passengers, especially as young as I was; sixteen. He may also have worried about me becoming scared after we got up in the air.

We settled into the seats and took off, climbed up then leveled. As I looked out, it seemed like we sat still. I leaned my head over the side of the plane. The wind hit me in the face so hard it jerked my head back. As I pulled my head back into the plane, I looked up-front and the pilot laughed. I smiled back. I guess he decided I wasn't afraid, so he climbed, doing small dives and flying in circles on one side then the other. It was such a thrill for me on my first ride. Bill and the guys all took short rides because, I think, they didn't want a girl showing them up. Then Bill took pictures of me beside the plane. As we headed back home, I couldn't believe what had happened.

It was many years later before I flew again. After we reared our four children I started to Wichita State and graduated with my degree in nursing at 48 years. Bill bought me a Cessna 150 for a graduation present. At age 50 I earned my pilot's license.

The grandkids soon expected me to take them up for short rides. They may have thought all Grandmas took their grandkids flying. I also loved doing stalls, so I would up by myself and fly around like a bird as I had dreamed as a child of five years. Also, Bill and I flew down to Oklahoma City Airport and did several touch-and-goes before we headed back home.

Bill was a white-knuckle passenger, especially with me. Never-the-less he wanted to fly to the Jefferson City Airport near where he grew up. We landed and visited his family who lived close by. Then we flew over the family farm, about 50 miles away, circled over a few times and headed back home.

Bill wasn't as air-worthy as I and decided not to get his license. I started my Master's Degree in nursing so after a few years we sold the plane. But that was all right because all my early childhood dreams had come true.

They included:

- Marry a good-looking man and have good-looking children; I did, and they were!
- Have two boys and two girls; I did!
- Be a nurse; I am.
- Fly an airplane; I did!

My childhood dreams came true, and many, many more!

## THOUGHT FOR THE DAY

Tom Elman

When I went to the playground as a kid, I liked the mood swings best.

Never forget about the "Law of Unintended Consequences."

You never lose. You either win or learn.

It's not what you gather that matters. It's what you scatter.

Real fisherman do not feel sorry for the bait.

Attitude is the difference between an adventure and an ordeal.

I don't believe in revenge, but accidents do happen.

I'm single by choice, but not necessarily by my choice.

Always try to remember that "stressed" spelled backwards is "desserts."

People that only work hard enough to not get fired, should be paid only enough to not quit.

Problems will happen during your journeys through life. Change your directions, not your destinations.

Death could be compared to playing with a Frisbee. When you die, your soul lands on the roof and it's "Game Over."

Giving money and power to the government is like giving beer and the car keys to teenagers.

When an old person dies, we lose a library.

A man's beliefs are his own affair, as long as they don't interfere with the liberty of others.

My hardest job today will be converting oxygen into carbon dioxide.

If your dog is fat, you are not getting enough exercise.

Is there a restraining order involved with any of the goals on your "Bucket List?"

"Caterpillars Rule." They eat a lot. Sleep for a while. Wake up beautiful.

## BOLDEA'S LAWS

### Don Boldea

1. You can be anything you want to be...
   - Regardless of gender;
   - Regardless of education;
   - Regardless of money.
2. If you want it...
   You have to work for it.
3. Never quit, never give up.
4. Always do your best.
5. Learn something new every day.
6. Aim high, challenge yourself.
7. Be honest, respectful and sensitive.
8. Be firm, be fair.
9. Never hold a grudge.
10. Love your spouse,
    love your children, love yourself.
11. Keep a sense of humor about all things.
12. Embrace, enjoy life.
13. "...To thine own self be true..."
14. Live by the Golden Rule...
    "Do unto others...
    as you would have them do unto you."
15. Believe in God, Love God, Pray to God.

## A STORM AND GRANDDAD'S HOUSE REMEMBERED

Beverly J. Hamilton

The year was 1948, and I had celebrated my eighth birthday in April. Spring had been filled with many blessings and one big challenge.

Our 160-acre farm in the southeast part of the county had been in the family since 1873 when Great Granddad homesteaded. Granddad built the current house in 1904 for his first wife. She and the child died in the home delivery. Two more wives would join him in that home each dying at an early age.

Now many years later my dad, an only child, lived in this same house with his wife and four children. I am the oldest. This year had been wet, and things had grown lush and plentiful. Our wheat crop looked to be abundant. The trees swayed heavy with new growth and lush foliage. The annual garden, planted on time, according to the Farmer's Almanac, was growing and promised to produce abundance for canning for next winter's pantry reserve. It was a lush year by any standard.

The challenge of that spring was mother developing asthma while pregnant with their fourth child. She had carried and delivered a premature infant son weighing five pounds two ounces, born May 2. They brought him home from the hospital, carried on a pillow, his resting place for the next few months.

We called him Little Joe. He was weak and nursing his bottle took a great deal of time. Mother would have me hold him and help with this task. He would finish and then it was time for another bottle! Grandmother would come sometimes and help. Mother was busy with the toddlers, two and three and a half. There were lots of responsibilities being a farmer's wife and mother. All the love and attention given little Joe, he thrived.

June found us approaching wheat harvest. Dad always used cutter crews coming up from south Texas in route to Canada cutting wheat as it ripened. The cutters would usually take three days at our farm.

That meant big meals with three to five extra mouths to feed. Mother was an excellent cook and always rose to the task with delicious nutritional meals and evening snacks to take to the field.

When harvest started it was work until dark every night, long hard days for all involved. This June morning was no exception. Upon rising Dad commented the sky remained dark to the northwest with a green cast. This worried him. Everything remained on schedule throughout the busy morning, but all were paying attention to the darkening of the sky to the northwest.

The sun shone bright on our farm, but the cutters worked feverishly to get the wheat cut and to the grain elevator in town. Conversation at the noon meal was serious, "we must hurry." We had electricity only a short time in our part of the county and outages from storms were still common.

Mother suggested we make extra bottles for little Joe. She asked me to gather blankets into the living room and tip over the big burgundy velvet chair on its side. Then I helped her tip over the matching couch. We were making a semi-protected area for the children to get under. We spread the blankets over the structure, covering where there were gaps where the furniture didn't quite meet. I added some toys to amuse the toddlers.

Mother kept a watchful eye out the widow as she continued to prepare food for the evening meal she would take to the field. The cutters would take turns stopping to eat. It was a race against time!

A little past 4:00 p.m. it began. First it was heavy rain with lots of lightning and thunder, and then the hail started.

"Get the children under the make shift tent," mother yelled.

That was my job. I placed Little Joe on his pillow in the corner of the overturned big chair. I instructed the toddlers to be quiet and play with their toy trucks.

There was a look of concern on all our faces. It was extremely loud in that old farm house with its long, narrow windows designed to let in lots of breeze to cool the house on hot days and nights in the summer months. Now the screens were ripping and curling from the hail as the wind blew the hail diagonally into the exposed glass panes.

Suddenly the dining room window broke, glass flying. Mother yelled for me to help her push the big Victorian buffet in front of the open window where the hail was pouring in on the floor. It was all we two could do to get it to even move but finally we succeeded.

Little Joe cried as the noise was loud and frightening. Mother voiced her concern for the men in the field hoping they had made it to cover in time.

The next three hours seemed like an eternity. The toddlers finally fell asleep, and I questioned if it would ever stop hailing. The constant roar sounded like a train passing by. At last it stopped, and the silence was equally loud!

We crawled out of our cramped safety chamber stretching and surveying the mess. It was dark outside when suddenly Dad came bursting in the back door. He was safe, and we were all alive unharmed and thankful! Dad was out of breath as he had run from the barn as soon as the hail stopped to see if his family was ok. He indicated there were drifts of hail everywhere like a mine field. It was dark, and the real damage would astound us upon daylight the following morning.

I remember it to this day as the most traumatic day of my young life. The day appeared like the dead of winter. The lush trees were stripped bare; the garden was a foot deep in garbage pounded into mush. The remaining wheat lay beaten into the ground like a herd of buffalo had passed through. The sun rose hot in a cloudless sky and the earth steamed and smelled sour and rotten. Drifts of hail insulated by layers of leaves and debris remained. All the windows on the north side of the house were smashed, broken glass everywhere. The screens had disappeared. The wood lap siding on Grandad's beautiful old farm house looked like a ball pin hammer had beaten it; the boards softened. The difficult task of clean up began.

The damages forced my dad to look for work at the local airplane plants to see his family through the following days and years ahead. Life on the farm continued for sixty-six more years. The family grew up and moved away pursuing their own lives. The hail scars and bruises remained on the old farm house, painted over twice in the ensuing years, forever to remind me of that dreadful hail storm as a child.

On a cold gray cloudy February day in 2014 the old farm house would stand empty and forlorn like an old soldier, to face the rising eastern sun one last time. The mood of the day was somber. Granddad's beloved one hundred-and ten-year-old house would face its last challenge, falling to the ground, a victim to progress and the wrecking ball. The old house had stood strong and served well providing shelter and refuge for many over the years. But its time on earth was finally over.

# GARDEN TIME

Sherry A. Phillips

When I grow weary of Gestapo step of Father Time, I take the stony path to where my garden cart waits. I sit with the sun to my back. Watch sweat bees flit throughout the tiny, blue flowers of cat mint.

The Sun's rays on purple salvia enhance its itchy-nose fragrance of sage. A Monarch lights on mown green fescue. I snip spent cone flowers.

Summer heat reminds me of my mother taking fresh peach pies from a hot oven. Pastry scraps: crisp, brown, dusted with sugar and cinnamon. A simpler time. Quiet goodness.

My backyard Eden gives respite from X-marked days and hen-scratched notes crammed between black calendar lines of days to come.

I breathe deep to fill my belly. Stretch arms heaven-ward and bask in the knowledge I have slowed the pace of time to the speed of a garden cart.

## JAMES

Caroline Grace

Now as a kid James was tall and thin,
No horned-rimmed glasses with his sheepish grin;
A coward at heart and fear within,
I guess that is why we all picked on him.

Most of us thought of James as a fool,
He was the funniest kid in school.
We even beat him up a time or two
Just to show James 'who was who.'

Now I work two jobs just to make ends meet;
Most of us work overtime just to eat.
Beneath the sun's hot, glaring heat
Or in the cold 'til we froze our feet.

But James owns a home in Malibu,
A ranch-style home with a mountain view.
Heaven's CEO of a company or two
I guess James showed us 'who was who!'

Memorial for James Stone
December 2017

# THE HIDDEN HOUSE

## E. L. Morrow

An access lane runs for about a mile off the main road. While leaving the blacktop, I observe the sign, "Private Road." I remember being here before and having the sense—well more like an assurance it's alright. Actually, I know I've been invited to this place—wherever it is. I know the place; been here before, but I can't remember when or why.

Each step becomes clear—just as I reach it. Similar to watching a movie I've seen before but can't remember how it ends. "Next, the main character opens the closet door; there is a dead body hanging on the back of the door, in a clear garment bag. But she doesn't notice because she is blind." OK, that example is from Wait Until Dark, but I still don't remember the ending.

Well, that's what this adventure is like. I remember just enough to reach the next step. I trust I'll know what to do then.

The lane has a new application of loose rock making the going slow. Soon the only sound to be heard is the crunch of the auto tires against the granite stones.

The path ends abruptly, with just enough room to turn a car around. Tall grass surrounds this parking area on all sides. I am glad I remembered to wear a jacket and closed shoes. The five-and-one-half foot tall grass has sharp edges, capable of slicing into the skin deeply enough to draw blood.

Despite my precautions, stepping into the grass brings stings and discomfort to my hands and fingers, as I push the blades aside to enter. I knew the slight pain would be worth the outcome. How did I know? Five steps and I find myself on the other side.

Some farmer has been planting this jungle like grass in a five-foot-wide band to discourage the uninitiated from finding the glorious beauty just beyond. The grass is cut each fall to supplement their animal feed during the colder months. But this being late April, everything, including the grasses are at their peak.

I step out of the grass and there it is. The first experience is the fragrance. Nearly two hundred different wildflowers live and bloom here each year. At any given time fifty to seventy-five will be flourishing. So, the aroma greeting a visitor is never the same from one day to the next. As something new blossoms, or the breezes shift the scents are combined differently.

Today it's a light and sweet smell that welcomes me. Daises, gladiolas, and gardenias combining with at least a dozen other nameless varieties—well, at least not a name known to me.

The second thing is the warmth. The sun on my face reminded me that soon the heat would prevent some of the wildflowers from blooming.

Finally, I am stopped in my tracks by the beauty. A bouquet of color that words cannot describe. The bright reds, yellows, and blues catch my eye first. But after a few seconds, the paler shades make their appearance: pastel yellows, pinks, salmon, oranges, cream and even some pale green blossoms. Small and delicate blooms announce themselves to my eye. Some flowers are so tiny: a magnifying glass is needed to see them. All nestled in foliage of greens, tans, mahogany, and shades in between.

Walking across the field of wildflowers and grasses takes about thirty minutes. My destination is a cluster of trees off to the left. Somehow this grouping of trees and undergrowth appeared different from other similar groups. It seemed a bit more, how can I describe the feeling? Perhaps more intentional—as if hiding some secret.

Once at the edge of the trees the undergrowth appears too dense to penetrate without a machete, or maybe a back-hoe? Then I spot what looks like a path, albeit for a rather short person. Crawling for only a couple feet, I find myself able to stand again. Square in front of me—not more than three yards away is an old house.

Only the front of the house is visible—the rest is shrouded in green growth of trees and vines. The front displays three doors separated by two windows. A covered porch runs across the front, with steps at the center rotted away. The railing looks to be four feet tall all around the outer edge of the porch including where the non-existent steps would have taken you. However, on the right side of the porch, someone had placed a full sheet of plywood. Positioned from the ground to the floor level creating a steep ramp—a rise of four feet to reach the porch level.

The plywood is a relatively new addition since it retains the color of lumber rather than the darkened weathered-wood-gray of the side walls and floor. Once on the porch, I try the first door.

An old-style screen door, with torn and rusting wire-mesh screen, opened with a creak. The door inside the screen is old and weather-beaten. Much paint has been applied over the years. The paint blistered and curled as if trying to escape the wood. The door was repainted numerous times apparently without removing much of the cracking and loose undercoats. Shades of green, gray, and some red paints have been lathered on liberally.

The doorknob was an old cheaper variety. It may have been shiny and bright when new, but all the luster or color had been worn away by thousands of hands over the years. Below the doorknob is an old-style keyhole requiring a skeleton key. None is available, and the door is securely locked, perhaps nailed shut from the inside.

Time to move on. Peering into the window affords a view of a darkened hallway, with two doors on the right side, and a staircase leading up the left side. The window proves impossible to budge.

The center door is modern. In fact, it is a pre-hung door with exterior storm door, locked from the inside. The new door is finished in dark blue with a golden door handle containing a thumb latch. Above the handle is a number keypad. This one too resists all efforts to open and enter.

Not enough time to try to guess the number combination, so I move on to the other window. I found this one utterly blacked-out as if a heavy black drape covers it from the inside. One last door to try.

This one is without a screen or storm-door and possesses no lock at all. Only a wrought iron handle similar to what you might find on some public restaurants—especially steakhouses. Giving a pull opens upon a large ballroom.

The room was recently in use. The walls are wood panels, with fancy inlay and decorative moldings. Reminiscent of what one might see in a movie set in the 1920s. The inlay pattern on the long wall to the right displays a male peacock with plumage fully displayed.

At the far end of the room is a raised platform containing a few folding chairs, some music stands, and a couple of snare-drums on stands. A baby-grand piano stands on the main floor next to the stage. Everything is clean; in fact, I detect a faint odor of furniture polish used on the wood surfaces.

The room seems impossibly large, so I step it off. The measurement is 40 by 60 feet. Hard to believe since the front of the house is barely 50 feet. No exits to the adjoining rooms can be observed. If connections are present, they are hidden in what appears to be a solid wall.

Again, I feel the whole place is familiar. I remember being here before. My children performed on that stage—singing, playing saxophone, flute, or in a melodrama from high school.

Over in that corner was the family gathering the year another cousin and I graduated from high school. And there is the entrance to the church where my father's funeral was held.

On the other side, the house I grew up in, and the streets I walked to and from elementary school. A few feet down the wall I see the bus stop for Junior High as we called it back then.

All this is confusing. How can all those things be in the same place?

What's that ringing? A telephone? No, it's the alarm clock. Oh, time to get up.

Now I remember this place. This is my hall of memories. I visit only in my dreams.

I must leave now. But I vow to return and discover what new or old memories might show themselves. I wonder what is in the other two rooms?

## BIKING ACROSS KANSAS

Rowena Hinshaw

We heard about BAK (Biking Across Kansas) for many years. But we still worked, and my husband didn't want to take a week off in June to go. We bike regularly around the city but not long rides. We were in our 60s, so it was time to go. Our 14-year-old grandson wanted to go, and had done many camping trips, etc. with us so he thought he could handle it. It worked out okay, and there were many good memories for him—seeing Kansas the slow way.

First, a little history of BAK. Larry and Norma Christie, of Wichita, Kansas started it in 1975. Less than 100 riders took part the first year. The annual event grew in the first five years, to several hundred riders. The route changes from year to year. It's still an eight-day bike ride from the west border to the east border.

In 2000, we tried the ride. We got our entry form. The cost was not high and included a detailed booklet of our daily schedule, a T-shirt, and some meals. To get to the starting point on Friday (before the ride started on Saturday) we rode a bus. A rental truck carried our bikes, clothes and bedrolls. The same bus took us home from the eastern Kansas border.

They also told us that Kansas was not FLAT, to expect hills, wind, and some rain. We would ride a certain mileage each day, at our own pace. Some young and experienced riders could finish the daily ride in a few hours. We always took the full day. The trip in 2000 was 475 miles. At end of each day we stayed in high school gyms, sleeping on the floor. Some riders preferred to camp at night in a tent as it was cooler sleeping outside. Showers were available, and there was time to repair bikes if needed We would have a group meeting at night and learn about any changes in the next day's ride. They carried all cyclists' gear to the next town each day. You couldn't arrive at the next town before noon as the gym might not be ready. We didn't have to worry about that as usually we were the last ones there. Our grandson could not ride the whole day, so he could ride ahead in the rental truck. Then he would unload all the bedding and clothes and get us a spot in the gym. We could leave each AM at 6:00-9:00.

This was a good experience, and we rode again in 2002. The ages of people riding ranged from the teens to 70s. Many older riders didn't ride the entire day. A lot of participants rode the BAK many times. People in the small towns we rode through were glad to see us as we would buy lunch and do some shopping.

The towns visited on the 2000 BAK trip included Goodland, Colby, Norton, Phillipsburg, Downs, Concordia, Blue Rapids and it ended in White Cloud at the Missouri river. This was the Northern route, but some years they do a Southern route.

## PETTY POI

Herbert Ingram

I eat my peas with honey

Been doin' it all my life

It makes the peas TASTE funny

But it keeps them on my knife.

## LIFE ON MARS

### Susan Howell

When I go to live on Mars
I will draw glyphs of distant stars
And make bricks with red sand and ice
And write poetry about all that is nice
About Mars.

I could be Poet Laureate of Mars
My adoring audience a chorus of bugs
I'd grow, so they'd be my friends,
But I'd eat those who didn't applaud.

Someday, someone will join me here
If a poet he be, we'll have to see.
A good poet he'd better not be.

## FARM MEMORIES

Debbi McGinn Elmore

I am not quite sure where my mother first conceived of the idea to share an Oreo cookie with our lead sheep, Blackie, but from that moment on she was hooked. She would often come to the door to bleat mournfully until Mom gave her another one.

At the time, my father and his father were jointly running an operation that not only included multiple farms but also cattle and sheep. When I was three, the Wichita Eagle sent a reporter to write a story about our 5,000 head of sheep. To this day I have the story and a photo showing me with some of the sheep, along with the near-genius quote, "I am not afraid of sheep," says three-year-old Debbi McGinn.

We put our sheep to pasture in one location until my dad deemed it was becoming overgrazed, then we moved all of them to a new grazing area. Sheep are docile animals, and all willingly follow their lead sheep. Unfortunately, the only person Blackie would follow was me, so at the age of five I was leading all 5,000 sheep down the road to new pasture. My dad would bring up the rear in his pickup, making sure no sheep wandered away.

I was not known for being shy about sharing my opinions, and one day I confronted my dad about the unfairness of walking miles down dusty country roads while he got to drive. He very nicely pointed out in return that Blackie would not follow anyone else, and without Blackie none of the 4,999 other sheep would budge. I was trapped with no recourse but to soldier on.

It really is a miracle my parents didn't disown me at some point as I was quite stubborn. One day I begged my dad to take me to cut the wheat with him, and he refused repeatedly, noting I would just change my mind when we got there, and he did not have time to shut down and take me back to our house. I begged and pleaded until he finally gave in.

Sure enough, after half an hour, I was tired of harvesting and wanted to go home. He refused to shut down and take me, so I just set off on my own through the wheat field, even though I was shorter than the wheat. He watched my little head disappear into the waves of gold and finally shut the combine off and came to find me. Needless to say, it was years before I "helped" with another harvest from the field side of things.

On the home side of things, Mom was noted far and wide for the lunches she would fix for the relatives and friends who came together to form the harvest crew each year. Special favorites among the men were her fried chicken and apple crumb crust pie. I loved the roast beef salad sandwiches and cinnamon sugar doughnuts she made from scratch. I don't think my sisters and I were as much help preparing the lunches as we thought, but we were definitely in the middle of the preparations. When the meal was ready, we would load it and drive to the field they were currently cutting. As soon as our car was spotted, the harvest crew would head in and enjoy the repast and cold drinks.

Mom was not just noted for her delicious food in the fields. When I was five, she became one of the founding members of the Halstead Hospital Auxiliary and would frequently take food for the physicians' luncheons. I grew up knowing that hospital very well.

My mom and her friend Betty were attending nurses' training at Halstead when they met two best friends from nearby Sedgwick, Dutch McGinn and Eugene "Zeke" Fry. They fell head over heels for the two farm boys with the result each couple served as the other's maid of honor and best man. Student nurses were not allowed to stay in training once they were married, so my mom and Betty gave up their careers. It was a year later when my lifelong friend Nancy and I were born, exactly seven weeks apart.

Earlier that same year, my dad's sister Janice and her husband Eugene McVicar had their second daughter, Janene, who arrived on Valentine's Day. So the three musketeers were born and have remained so to this day, going all the way through grade school and high school in the same class.

When we were old enough, we would ride our bikes to town for the day. Nancy was the furthest south, and I would be waiting for her when she arrived at the end of our lane. We then rode on together while Janene headed into town from the east. We would go to the library, the drugstore, play at the park, or just hang out with other classmates we ran into.

From the time I learned to read and write, I loved to do both. On many occasions I rode my bike to town and spent the afternoon selecting and then checking books out at the library. When I got home, I would read all of them and repeat the process the next day.

When I wasn't engrossed in a book, I was busy creating and writing stories, all featuring the same three characters: Janene, Nancy and me. I lacked drawing skills, so I would illustrate my stories by tracing pictures out of comic books.

Mom was from eastern Colorado, and that is where our maternal grandparents, aunt, uncle and cousins lived. Because Dad was a farmer/stockman, he could never be away from home longer than one day. We spent many holidays in the car going to Colorado early, spending the day with family, and driving home through the night. Dad would drive with the light on, so I could read. I didn't realize at the time how difficult that must have been.

We also enjoyed spending time at area lakes and Joyland, the amusement park in south Wichita. Once a year Joyland would hold Scholarship Day, and students poured in from all over south central Kansas to exchange their good grades for free tickets. I frequently took my friends as guests. One day we were riding the roller coaster, and I was holding the tickets down with my foot since I didn't have any pockets. We hit one rough patch, and the tickets went flying off into space. That was the end of our rides for the day.

Life on the farm offered its own rewards and challenges, much of it dependent on the weather. In the years where there was a flood, early frost, a late freeze, a hail storm or drought, we didn't have any crops to speak of so money was tight. In those tight years, Mom worked as a nurse's aide at the hospital and Dad took winter jobs at Cessna Aircraft, like many of the other farmers in our area.

Dad was the quintessential Irishman, with boisterous good humor and helpfulness that drew others to him. When I was in junior high, he would entertain the high school boys with his "philosophies on life" and they loved it. I thought it was great that he was so popular the older boys just flocked to our farm.

As farm kids, all of us learned to drive early. When we got our restricted licenses at 14, we had already been driving farm vehicles on our respective acres for years. Also, as farm kids, we had the most leeway with our licenses, as we could drive to and from school and also on farm errands. Farm errands in a small town can cover a wealth of activities since no one really knew if we were picking up seed or buying groceries.

Mom never gave up on her dream of becoming a nurse. When I was a freshman, she went to see Sister Carmel at the St. Joseph Hospital School of Nursing in Wichita (the school at Halstead had closed several years earlier). She asked Sister to consider relaxing the ban on married student nurses. Sister Carmel told her if she could pass a test with 90% or better, she would let her back into school. Mom took it and passed with a 98% score! Thus did she and Betty return to school and go into nursing as full-time careers. I will never forget how hard she worked, spending all day in classes and working the floors in the hospital, then coming home to cook and clean for all of us.

I have always counted myself fortunate to have grown up in a small town where everybody knew everybody else. The smaller schools we attended meant we could participate in nearly any activity we chose. We were involved in band, music festivals, speech contests, dramatic interpretations, scholastic competitions, pep club, Student Council, the annual musical and the yearbook staff. Having all those opportunities to excel gave us a measure of self-confidence we carried into our futures after high school.

## OUR DADDY'S RIGHTEOUS ANGER

Sharon Revell

"Get out and don't bother me anymore." My father straightened up, brandishing the machete he had been using to chop down weeds. His dark eyes, inherited from his Cherokee grandmother, flashed with anger. I'm sure the two men standing on the sidewalk that balmy summer evening in the 1940s hoped they could escape unscathed. They wished they had never stopped to ask their neighbor to join the organization closest to their hearts, the local chapter of the Ku Klux Klan.

Daddy was not a big man, close to 6 feet tall but thin all his life. He had high cheekbones and wavy black hair; my mother had thought him very handsome. Her parents were not as thrilled. His Cherokee ancestry was not a trait to be proud of; many worried that Native Americans consorted with blacks. My grandfather was pretty sure they did "those dances" as a way of working themselves up to sexual conquest. And his upbringing on the streets of Wichita after his mother left for another man, taking the girls but leaving the three boys with their father, did not match up to a family whose ancestors had fought in the American Revolution.

Nevertheless, they married in 1930 and were immediately plunged into the depression that engulfed the United States. Somehow, they survived. And my mother had fond memories of their Saturday morning trips to the library for free books to entertain them until Monday when they would return to the grind of living. Sometimes, though, my father would have to pick up the books, because my mother's shoe soles were too thin to walk across the bridge to town. They could not spare a nickel for the cobbler to re-sole her only pair of shoes.

Eventually life became easier, and I was born in 1935. My grandma was very relieved that, although I had big ears and a bald head, I was white. It was the hottest dust bowl summer ever. Air conditioning was an unimaginable fantasy for the future, and they did not even have an electric fan. Many evenings, they slept in the side yard of their old apartment house because their second-floor apartment was unbearable. But my dad had found a steady job with a pay check every week. They did not mind walking everywhere they went. And my mother had learned to make nutritious (if not delicious) meals from practically anything. Besides, they were in love.

It was a thrill when they could move to a little rental house down the street from Lawrence Stadium, with a fenced back yard and a tree in the front. Grass did not grow there, and I remember playing in the dust during the summers. But mother planted a little bed of purple vinca, and Daddy kept everything strong enough to grow there neatly trimmed.

I don't know where he got the machete he was using and regretfully, we lost it in later years. But the memory of our daddy's righteous anger lives on in family lore.

*Starla Criser*

# CELEBRATING KANSAS CITY ROYALS 50th ANNIVERSARY

## Maudyne Cline

Here we go again, another game and few home runs.

The Kansas City Royals may go down in baseball history as the team who lost 100 games in one season.

Come on, guys, stop, think, listen, take a big breath, knock the dirt off your shoes, spit out your sunflower seeds. Ready or not it's your turn to bring your buddy in from second base.

You remember you brought Joe in your rotation last night from third base.

Rest up now, as the team has five days off, and then you can watch the baseball All Star Game

The State of Kansas and the Kansas City area are proud of their baseball team who has been around these past fifty years and the team is still having fun, me too!

# THERE I STOOD

## Don Boldea

There I stood.
With a fresh, warm cup of coffee in hand.
The slight chill of night air was intensifying
My senses.

There I stood.
Staring out into the dark, quiet, open expanse
Of nature as it presented itself.
You could hear the dew as it welled up
On every blade of grass, and on every leaf
Of the trees.

There I stood.
Swallowing a sip of my coffee, the
Silence of night was now being interrupted.

There I stood.
A soft, warm, gentle breeze rustled the leaves;
Birds began singing their morning songs, these are all things
That make up the sweet sounds of Dawn's approach.
There I stood.
I stood in awe and wonder of the enchantment of a new born day.
My senses refreshed by the transition from dark to dawn.

There I stood.
My coffee now gone, I am once again
At peace with the world, life, and the
Balance of nature.

# THE MULBERRY TREE

## Bonnie Lacey Krenning

The boys are climbing the mulberry tree, picking the big, juicy berries and eating 'em. Now they're throwing some down so I can pick 'em up and eat 'em. They are so juicy and sweet as sugar! I want to climb the tree, too.

My big brothers tell me "No, 'cause you might fall! Mom don't want you to show yer bloomers."

I can hold on like my brother about my size and I'd like to wear overhalls like the boys do. I think I will climb the mulberry tree sometime.

I wake up smelling the good breakfast Mom was fixing; hot biscuits and gravy. We all eat a big breakfast because Daddy and the boys are going out in the fields today to hoe the corn and 'taters. Then they leave, and Mom washes the dishes. When I get bigger I will help her. Mom says I just had a birthday and now I am three years old. But I'm too little to help. I want to get bigger soon.

I run outside and don't see Daddy and the boys anywhere. I will climb the mulberry tree today. Climbing is really hard. It's hard to hold on around the tree 'cause it's so big. My arms and legs are so short and my dress tail git's in the way. Now it's better 'cause I can use the limbs to git up into the middle of the tree where the berries are. The berries are sweet, and the juice is running down my arms. It's cool up here 'cause it's still morning and the sun is not hot yet.

Mom is calling me!

"Bonnie Mae, wher' are you?"

Why is she yellin' at me? She only says "Bonnie Mae" when she's mad at me! Why is she so mad at me? She sounds so scared! I holler back,

"I'm up in the mulberry tree!"

She's hollerin' back, "What?"

Why is she yellin' so loud? Here she comes, hurrying! She's trying to run fast!

She's still yellin'! "What are you doin' up in the tree? Be careful or you'll fall! Git down! Be careful! Don't catch yer dress tail or you might fall! Little girls are not supposed to climb trees! You're showin' yer bloomers! Little girls like you are not supposed to show their bloomers!"

I asked, "Why can't I wear overhalls?"

She says, "Girls are not supposed to wear boy's clothes. It's not ladylike."

I wonder what ladylike means, but I don't ask. I start to climb down. Why is she so mad and sounds scared too?

Mom is underneath the tree now. She says, "Yer not supposed to go where I can't see you! Why are you climbin' trees?"

I tell her, "I saw the boys climbin' trees yesterday and they wouldn't let me climb 'cause I would show my bloomers. They're out workin' where they can't see my bloomers. So now I can climb and eat the mulberries."

As I git to the ground Mom takes me by the hand and leads me to the big flat rock by the well. It's where she has me sit when she's mad at me. That's better than getting' a spankin' like the boys do sometimes.

She tells me, "Sit down here on the rock 'til I tell you git up! Don't move! I want to see you from the kitchen window while I'm cookin' dinner! I want you to think about what you did."

I still don't know why she is so mad at me, and so scared! Why can't girls do what boys do? I don't want to be a boy. I just want to do what boys do like climbing trees, riding horses and getting haircuts.

Mom had me sit on the rock once before. It was when Daddy cut the boys' hair but wouldn't cut mine. It got so tangled and hurt when

Mom combed it. So, when Daddy cut the boys' hair I watched where he put the scissors. When they left and I was alone, I cut my hair. I heard Mom calling my name and I crawled under the bed. When she saw my hair in the floor she yelled "Bonnie Mae!" As I started to crawl from under the bed she started crying. She set me on the stool and trimmed my hair. She looked sad and took me by the hand, took me to the big flat rock and made me sit for a long time.

Now I've been sittin' here for a long time for climbing the mulberry tree. Now Daddy and boys are comin' in from the fields for dinner. Mom says I can git up and come into the kitchen to eat with them. I see Daddy and the boys are sweaty and dirty. I don't want to get so sweaty, but I still want to wear overhalls, ride horses and climb trees. But I'm glad I don't have to hoe corn and 'taters.

## KANSAS WHEAT HARVEST EVOLVED THROUGH THE DECADES

Debbi McGinn Elmore

Harvest - a time when farmers and their families could rejoice in the fruits of their labor, or shake their heads in sadness at whatever calamity of nature had destroyed them. A time of hard work, but of community, as neighbors and family came together to help each other.

As one of 14 children growing up on a farm outside Durham, Kansas, Henrietta "Hanky" Thomas remembers every family member pulling his or her share during harvest. While the men and boys worked in the fields, the women and girls took over feeding livestock, doing chores, milking the cows and cooking for those in the field. Everything in those days (the 1930s and 40s) was further complicated by the lack of running water and electricity. To harvest the wheat, everyone in their area used a combine pulled by a tractor. Her family owned the only thresher, so their neighbors for miles around would bring their grain to be thrashed. As grain went into the granary for storage, the children would get in and push the grain back.

"After the grain was thrashed, the men would have a meeting and then we would have homemade ice cream," Hanky recalls. "It was the only time each year we had a chance to have ice cream."

Glenn Bell's family wasn't so lucky. They farmed outside Oxford, Kansas with a team of horses, and no one in the area owned a thresher. They would cut the wheat with a binder, then gather the stacks of wheat, oats and alfalfa to wait for the traveling thresher to visit. That thresher was a forerunner to today's custom cutters, who travel through several states cutting wheat. "I remember when the first combines came to Kansas in the 1940s," Glenn recalls.

In Glenn's case, the women spent most of the day cooking, but the men came in from the field to eat. They always bought ice so the men could have iced tea. The men carried their water to the fields in vinegar jugs wrapped in wet burlap to keep it as cool as possible.

Fast forward to a time when combines were self-propelled, but had not yet morphed into the self-contained behemoths of today. The farm children of the 30s and 40s had become parents themselves, and their children continued the traditions of harvest.

"Wheat harvest was the busiest time of the year," explained Nancy Fry Stahl and her mother, Betty Fry. "Not only were we harvesting wheat, but there was preparing fields for fall crops, gardening and of course cooking for the field crews. Mornings started out early, preparing the food for lunch, which would be delivered to the field where the men were working. This meal was usually substantial and hardy. Evening or afternoons we would take a lighter meal. Noon meal usually was fried chicken, another meat dish, fresh vegetables from the garden, mashed potatoes and a couple of different salads, fresh bread and butter, homemade cakes and pies, and lots of cold water and ice tea. Preparing the water jugs was quite a process; in the early days we used glass jugs and wrapped them up in burlap that had been soaked in cold water to keep them cool in the field."

"My younger brothers started helping with the harvest almost as soon as they were able to drive a tractor by themselves, and a lot of the times they were working the fields a few miles away preparing them for planting all alone, at the age of 9 or 10," Nancy adds. "True story about one of my brothers operating the combine in a field by himself, while Dad was hauling wheat to the elevator, and the combine caught fire. It could have been a huge disaster, but all worked out. I remember one year, Dad and I were cutting wheat west of Sedgwick, Kansas, when a tornado went over the field. It did not touch down and did not do any damage, but Dad and I crawled under the big wheat truck and hid out until it passed on by."

Like other farm children, Nancy got a restricted driver's license at the age of 14 and began driving the harvest truck to town. Prior to that, she enjoyed rides to town perched on top of the grain in the back of the harvest truck, as did many of the younger farm children.

On many farms where there were not yet any boys, the girls would work as harvest hands. Tractors and combines did not have air-conditioned cabs in those days, so it was hot, dusty work that could be dangerous.

"We had terraces for more controlled drainage," recalls Janene Schroeder. "We planted wheat on those terraces as well. The wheat was quite tall compared to the short wheat of today. We had a lot of rain, so weeds covered the ground. It was hard to tell the really wet spots. It was scary to cut wheat on the side of a terrace because the combine tipped sideways. You sat pretty high on a combine and then I just sunk. I tried to get out, but was buried. Dad got the biggest tractor we had, but had a difficult time getting to the combine because he didn't want to drive over uncut wheat. I was finally pulled out and Dad said we would wait to cut close to the terraces and save that until last."

Rain brought its own problems as equipment would get stuck. It also posed delays for the custom cutters who adhered to a fairly rigid schedule to move through the various states as the wheat ripened.

"I remember two harvests when they had their first 4 wheel drive John Deeres," says Mark McGinn, speaking about J & M Custom Cutters. "We had a lot of rain one year and it was already about the 10th of July and they had to move on north. So they wallered my wheat out of the 80 west of town and then went over to my uncle Jerry's 40 acres out in the middle of that section and wallered it out, flushing out ducks from standing water in the process."

As the children of the 1950s and 1960s grew up and married, a new generation of children was born. Many of those now lived in town, but the thrill of harvest was still very real to the ones lucky enough to live in the country, even if their parents had other jobs and no longer worked on the farms. One of those children was Dr. Ryan Currier, now a radiologist in Louisville, Kentucky, who remembers his excitement at riding with his grandfather during harvest.

"We loved the wheat harvest. With one glimpse of my grandpa's silver combine, my brother, sister, and I would be outside watching.

Our mom would lead us out into the field as we all tried to flag him down. My brother, sister and I would jump up and down trying to grab his attention. If he didn't see us the first time, we would watch in despair as the combine disappeared behind a giant cloud of dust and shooting straw. That feeling would go away as soon as he turned around and we started the next round of jumping and yelling. Once he saw us, he would pull over and we would join him. We would run over to the combine. Our grandpa would be looking down smiling, always in a mesh hat and pocketed t-shirt. We'd climb up the ladder to join him. It was a climb that seemed 30 feet high at the time. Once aboard, one of us would be on Grandpa's lap driving, and the other plastered against the front windshield watching the carnage below.

We called it 'chomping.' The combine would pull in all the wheat, chew it up, and it would disappear into the 'mouth' of the machine. I'm not sure how long we would actually ride with him, but it never seemed long enough. We could have stayed in there for hours. I relive that memory every time I drive past a wheat field or see a combine. It's one of those childhood memories that brings a little smile to your face every time you think about it."

## A BUTTERFLY LANDED SUDDENLY

Martha Williams Prentice

A butterfly landed suddenly upon my shoulder;
  I sensed it more than felt it,
    I barely saw the movement of it,
      in a corner-of-my-eye look.
My attention was solely focused on the drama
  that unfolded from the pagers of my book.

I gave it all the time I thought it wanted
  to preen and rest its delicate fluorescent spans
    closed now then spread, and folded again—
I think I felt the stir it caused, didn't I?

The book, now closed, I slowly laid beside me,
  content to wait and see what was to come.

After a while the butterfly
  lifted up and out a ways,
    in front of me at center stage,

to set the scene for one pristine performance.
   It flitted here, and darted there,
      first high, then low it swooped the air.
I heard and felt the melody, the tempo of its prance;
   floral scent was spread upon me
      by its fluttered dance,
         and took me to a place of pure delight.

I couldn't pull my eyes away,
   I wanted to watch forever,
    but then it flew above the shrubs,
          and way beyond the fence.
Motionless, I sat there, waiting, wanting, wanting more.

Then here it came—I smiled out loud.
   I even gave a sigh,
    to thank this lovely creature
      that is far more than meets the eye.

How did it know, this butterfly,
   who I was or where I was;
   it came to me, I'm sure, with purpose,

   did I receive the message?
This time, it came in high
  then floated down
  and circled round me there.
I knew the encore was ending,
  goodbye was sweet and fleeting;
  a covert wind moved in
  and swept it up
    to direct it in its journey.

I picked up my book, turned to the path,
  and this day walked the long way home,
  looking back once to remember
    that place, that time, that encounter
      meant just for me.

## LOLA

Bunnie Clark

I suppose many people might associate red with Christmas: The garland wrapped around the snow-tipped tree branches, the little train running circles under the tree on its miniature track and, of course, the teddy bear with the Santa cap on its head.

But not me! When I think of red, I think of my Mother when wearing her Bright Red Lipstick. My Mom was a Cherokee Indian. She was a tall, striking woman. Black hair and high cheek bones caused people to turn and look. I was so proud of my Mom when she came to my grade school. The kids were like, "ooh, is that your Mom? She is pretty."

My Mom may have looked like an angel, but she was not. She was feisty and opinionated. She laughed easily and was always ready to tell a joke on herself. But don't let that ready SMILE SNOW you. She could turn on a dime, and any of her seven children could feel the switch on our backside or the sting of her sharp words. But her temper was short lived. We were treated to her laugh more often than not.

******

The pictures I have of my Mother tell her story. The earliest picture I have was probably in the early 20s. No flappers, there. Evidently it was the norm to be sober and unsmiling (except for one mischievous looking little girl) in these pictures. Looking at the surroundings in the picture, I would venture to say there was not much of a reason to smile. My grandmother, a full blood Indian woman, was seated in a chair with a child, Virgil, on her lap and two little girls standing on each side of her chair.

Lola and Louise were the names of the girls and Virgil the youngest son. There would soon be another child, one who would be called Lorene. My Mom, Lola is standing behind her: her elbow propped on the chair with her chin cradled in her hand. She must have been about seven. Lucille, the oldest daughter was already long gone. Lucille had married and left home for a better life, at least that was her hope. There were also two older brothers, Eugene and Bruce. Lola, my Mother, is the middle child. The girls were wearing light colored dresses, and all were barefoot. Virgil was wearing a long dress that baby boys wore. Grandmother had on long light-colored stockings. The girls had straight hair bobbed just below their ears. The background is a shabby looking yard that you would expect to see a couple of hens scratching around. The picture is one you would might see in a magazine taken by a photographer who wanted the world to know about their plight. Sadly, there was no one to tell their story but me. And, of course, I see it through a different lens. It is a mystery to me who took the picture, and anyone who could tell me has long since passed away.

******

What happened between the years of that picture, and the one I have of her when she was 16 were hard times for the family. Grandmother died when My Mother was nine. They split apart the family. They sent my Mother, two of her older brothers and the youngest brother to an Indian boarding school in Tahlequah, Oklahoma. It was no time at all before the two oldest boys ran away from there. They left two younger girls with relatives, one just a baby and the other crippled with a clubfoot. Mom and Virgil were there alone. They separated the boys from the girls. They were forbidden to speak any Cherokee. Mother forgot her native language by the time she left the boarding school. Oh yes, one word, she did remember, and she used it often. It was the Cherokee word for Fart.

My Mother defied rules and regulations. Her fiery and free spirit was on display shortly after they boarded her. Mom would go to the fence that separated the boys and girls in the playground. She would call to her brother. They would hold hands through the fence until play time was over. Eventually, my Mother flaunted the rules completely and would take Virgil from his dorm to her own. He walked the halls with her. She was determined no one would separate them. For whatever reason, they tolerated her fierce protectiveness towards her brother.

Being sent to that boarding school gave my Mother a reprieve through the school year. During summer and holidays, they sent the children home. Her Father was a drinker and an abuser of his family. He abused them with little provocation. There are hints of sexual abuse. A few years before Grandmother died, she became ill and went to bed and stayed there until she died. I often wonder if it was depression that sent her there. My Mom would brush her Mother's long hair after she came home from school. The children would gather around her bed, play the piano and the banjo and sing. Those were the good times my Mother would talk about. I could hardly get her to tell me much about the bad times.

******

But back to the picture of her at age sixteen. She's posing by the side of a brick building. She's trying to put her best foot forward. It's a happy picture. Her head is thrown back, and she is smiling big. Her school uniform was a light-colored shirt and dark pants. Her scarf is blowing out with the wind. I smile when I look at the picture because she had chosen to stand by a drain pipe that spills water onto a concrete block. She is standing on the block. I am speculating that the reason the picture was taken there was because the block gave a good place to stand. I see the attitude in her bearing. That's my Mom.

Lola played ball, took ballet lessons and sang. There was even a Girl Scout troop at the school. Mom loved the school. Even when her voice grew hoarse and rough from her years of smoking, she would still sing the songs she sang learned at boarding school. And she loved playing baseball. Years later, she coached all her kids for their summer ball games. Even me, although she always laughed about how I jumped over the ball instead of trying to catch it.

When she was in her sixties, she was sitting on the bleachers babysitting her grandchildren while my two sisters played ball. They needed a player in the outfield. They convinced Mom she could fill in. There wouldn't be any action out there. Well, as it turned out, there WAS some action out there. While Mom crouched down, waiting for a ball to come her way, she felt a tug on her pants. Looking down was one of the grandchildren. "Grandma, we have to go to the bathroom." Mom loved to tell that story.

But, it was baseball and my Mother's audacious behavior that was her downfall. It was a traveling team. She met a guy somewhere on one of those trips. His name was Joe. That's all I know. He was my

Father. I doubt he ever even knew my Mom was carrying his child. When it became obvious that she was pregnant, they sent her home. Back to the big old farmhouse in the country. My grandfather did not have a car. He had a wagon and two horses. Long after Mom left home and had children, he still had the horse and wagon. We used to ride into town with Grandpa when we went to visit. That was the only fun and exciting part of visiting him.

I was born in the Claremore Indian Hospital. Mom was there for quite some time before I was born. I don't know how long, but long enough that she adored the nurses who took care of her until I was born. She named me after one of the nurses and her oldest sister.

Mom met a man by the name of Paul. She was isolated out there in the country, but somehow, she got around. She married Paul. Her mother-in-law quickly annulled the marriage. I mean, you can't be married to an Indian woman with an illegitimate child and be a respectable person. So, it's back home with Grandpa. Both her sisters were home, too. I imagine the three were a handful for their dad.

We skip a few years ahead to the picture of my Mom and the man who she eventually married. She is wrapped in an Indian blanket with a headdress on. They've moved to the big city now where they will start their own family. Like I said, Lola was a beautiful woman. She attracted men. (All her life.) My dad was so enamored of Mother that in order to see her, he would skate on frozen creeks and rivers to court her. He lived in a town a few miles away. Once he got there,

Granddad would knock him off the porch with a broom. I guess Granddad finally gave up, because they married and eventually had seven more children. Two of the seven were twins. Sadly, one died after only a few weeks.

******

Mom's oldest brother became known as Chief Parris. He followed carnivals and would enter boxing fights to make money. Eventually, he became the one other fighters would try to defeat. As Chief began to make money and gain recognition, he found a way to get his brothers and sisters to the Big City. Chief fought his way into the big time. He became the southwest champion of the welterweight and middleweight division. His signature outfit before he entered the ring was an Indian headdress and blanket. Naturally, we all wanted to wear that outfit. There is a picture of me in a blanket and headdress when I am four or five years old. He was forever in our lives, even now. Just type Chief Parris into Google, and there he is.

Uncle "Chico" as we called him, passed away in 1993. By that time, only he and my Mother still lived. She was always special to him. His two other sisters, Louise and Lorene had also died when they were young and left no children. Mom's youngest brother, Virgil, was a tail gunner in World War 11. He was killed. He left behind a wife and two little girls. After his wife was murdered, those girls went to live in California with their grandmother. As the years went by, we lost contact with them. That left Mom's children. We became his "favorites."

It wasn't until I was older that I realized how much Mom had suffered through the years. Her ancestors (in the not too distant past) had survived the Trail of Tears. It was the hardy stock from which she came that keep her going through her own private losses. I seldom saw my Mother cry even though she certainly had plenty to cry about.

I was born during the later years of the Great Depression. Our family never had much in the way of material possessions. Dad was a hard worker and a hard drinker. Paychecks didn't always make it home. Mom managed to keep us fed and dressed. Once Uncle Chief gave her money to buy a dress. She didn't buy a dress; she bought groceries instead. When Chief came to town, he would tell her to put on her new dress. "We are going dancing." Mom told him the dress was at the cleaners. The nonexistent dress was a symbol to me of Mother's resilience and ability to laugh when there was plenty of reason to cry.

Mom wrote her own story called Mournful Winds. Her Indian forebears of the Trail of Tears left a legacy. Mom is part of the legacy.

Starla Criser

# AN UNFINISHED STORY

Mournful Winds

By Lola

*This story was unedited and printed just the way Bunnie Clark's mother had written it.*

There have been many mournful winds through the years of my life causing rivers of tears to be shed…especially when darkness comes. One thing I've learned; hurting is always worse at night.

Being born an Indian was the first blow life dealt me. I wasn't born a coal miners' daughter, nor did I wear a coat of many colors like two famous country and western singers. I was born an Indian. In those days, Indians weren't accepted by the rest of society.

Our race was the cause of a lot of harassment, but we children didn't know we were different. Going to public school was a heart break. I cried a lot on the way home not understanding why I was treated differently. My mother, a full blood Cherokee, would hold me tight and try to soothe the hurt away. She would tell me those who said cruel things didn't understand that God had put different types of people on the earth. My mother was a full blood Cherokee, educated at the Indian Seminary at the Cherokee Capitol of Tahlequah, Oklahoma. After graduation, she taught music in a local school. She was considered "rich" as she owned some land, two homes and had oil rights from the Indian land allotments. My father was a half Cherokee and half Scots-Irish from Nowata County, Indian Territory. He had been told of a pretty and rich Indian girl who was teaching school in Tahlequah. What romance they might had I never knew but they married and moved to Salina, Ok.

My mother owned a home in Alluwe and one in Pryor, which were not elaborate but very comfortable. She also owned a farm and my parents went into the Poland China Hog business and also did some farming. There were eight children, four boys and four girls. I was the fifth of the seven who survived into childhood.

In the early days there were parties at our house. The guests consisted of farm neighbors, aunts and uncles and lots of cousins. There was music and square dancing and laughter. In those days, everyone played something musical—my brothers included—so the music came easy. We younger children stood back and watched the fun until it was time for us to go to bed. Then my Mother and other women would cook all night on our wood cook stove.

At Christmas the same people would come again. A large tree would have been cut down and, standing in the corner of our living room, would have been decorated with popped corn and red berries, called red haws, that grew on our farm. We also had walnut and pecan trees, so needless to say, there was a lot of fudge and divinity, chock full of nuts.

At Easter time the "big pasture" would be full of colored eggs that we children gathered eggs for hours. (Even months afterwards, sometimes, we would still find a brightly colored eggs as we were picking wild flowers or driving the cows in to be milked) The big question for us children "where did the colored eggs come from?" After we were snug in our beds the surprise was done, put in place and we never saw them being colored.

Our father had been a U.S. Marshall in the Indian Territory. Many times, old-timers, friends of his that he had sent to prison, came to our home and they would talk far into the night about the fun of the chase and of the escapes some had made. One man named Boy Ice, had escaped from the Nowata jail. My Dad asked how he managed that he said he would never tell: he would go his grave with that secret. Of course, while they talked, we kids were in our beds but were listening to every exciting tale.

Dad kept his U.S. Marshal badge in his sock and handkerchief dresser drawer. We children could look at it, but were never allowed to touch it. (He had the same rule about his Stetson hats.) But Pete, a child who practically lived with us took the badge and wore it in Alluwe. A friend of Dad's saw him and told him that Mose would beat him if he found out he had it. Pete got scared and threw it away and would never tell where.

We should have been happy.

But our father was a drunkard. He went through our mother's money investing in "deals" that fell apart because he drank and ran around. He wasn't much of a husband.

Some hard times followed.

I was 9 years old when my mother took to her bed with an illness: a very long illness, that we never did learn the true nature of. Mama never went to a hospital. The one doctor would make house calls. A bed was moved into the front room and for the full time of her illness that is where she stayed.

She was always able to talk to us not never got out of bed up until a couple of days before her death. That day she felt good enough to sit in a chair. My sister brushed her long black hair and, for fun, put make up on her. We kids thought that was funny. We laughed a lot because she never wore make up. She was very pretty, we all told her, thinking Mama was going to get well. She laughed and talked with us and then went back to her bed. After that, she didn't know much or talk anymore.

Then she left us.

Our world was turned upside down. My Dad could no longer keep the seven children together so, in twos, we were sent in all directions, separated forever. Our mother's death was not the final blow. Separation was a terrible thing to happen to a bunch of very young children who loved one another.

The two older brothers, Chief and Bruce, were sent to the Chilocco Indian school for a short time and then to Sequoyah Indian School. Chief soon left to seek his fortune and became a prize fighter. He went all over the U.S., Mexico and Canada too. Years would go by without us seeing him. We did keep in touch but not often. Bruce also left and worked different jobs on his own. One older sister, Lucille, got married. The two-year-old baby, Lorene was taken by Dad's sister to Grove, OK. Transportation was such that we didn't see her from that time until she was 10. Loise was too young to go to school and she was the only one to stay at home.

My youngest brother, Virgil, and I were enrolled in the Sequoyah Indian School for the five civilized tribes located near Tahlequah.

Ironically it was the very same school my mother had attended only then it was the Seminar for Indians.

The school was for Indian children of the Cherokee, Choctaw, Chickasaw, Seminole and Creek tribes. They had to be of a certain Indian degree and a half orphan. Our enrollment made my brother and me a part of the 350 students who were kept there year-round. As one class graduated more young were taken in. Occasionally we had some that would join in higher classes, not many.

We were scared and very lonely coming from a big family that had suddenly been yanked apart and sent in all directions. My brother was sent to one side of the campus and I to the other. I broke the rules many times by going to the boy's side to find and talk with my little brother who was only seven.

As a nine-year-old, I was placed in the Administration Building which had dormitories, as well as the main office, and was where a few employees also lived. I stayed until high school when I moved to Cherokee Hall and lived in a room with a roommate.

The school taught us much. We had all the conveniences of the modern world. We had good caring teachers that were interested in our education. We were offered so much and it was up to us individually to make of ourselves what we wanted to be.

We were trained military style from the beginning. Those that didn't have what we called detail: kitchen, dining room or farm and dairy or hospital-were awakened by bugle all. We fell into our company, marched to the football field and did a lot of calisthenics exercises.

Then back to make our beds and get ready for breakfast. Then our day started. We all had a detail that lasted ten weeks and then we changed. That was to teach many different jobs.

When May at last came, our school days were over for summer vacation. Those that were fortunate enough to have homes went there for the summer and came back the first of September, starting all over again. For three years I cried for my family. Then I finally knew that I was all I had, wit the exception of my little brother that I still had with me. We were there for ten years.

Virgil learned the Indian languages by association, playing and working with the boys from different tribes. As for me, we were taught English in our home from both parents. Only English was spoken in school, on order of the staff of Indian Interior Affairs, even though we had many come to our school who could speak nothing but their own tongue. But the matrons (as they were called) would clap their hands and make them stop. By the time they were young teens they had forgotten their own tongues.

This is where my Mother's story ended. She did have some notes at the end, so I believe she intended to write more. Some of the notes: *Girl Scout song leader Oklahoma All Indian School, Usher for Eleanor Roosevelt; was selected to go to Sweden. Neither turned out. Was a tap dancer, ballet dancer, played basketball, baseball, was in every musical program, no instruments, just sang.*

## I WAS WALKING BAREFOOT
### Donita M. Davis

I was walking barefoot in my kitchen one day,
(I knew I should have worn shoes)
When I stubbed my little toe on the table leg.
Let me tell you, that was very bad news.

T'was ag-o-my, unadulterated pain.
There was no way to hide it.
And all I could do was tape it to
The toe that lay beside it.

"That's how it is in life," I mused,
Sitting down to philosophize.
"You just need to do what you know to do."
Now ain't that statement wise!

## THE LOVE OF A CHILD

## Ann Alvis

I endured a lot of heartache and pain growing up and becoming an adult. Life, it doesn't ask you what you want. You wake up every morning to see what it offers you.

It had been two weeks. On a hot summer morning, when I woke up to find my husband, the love of my life had gone to be with the Angels in heaven, yet it felt like yesterday.

I found it was hard to smile or laugh anymore. Life, I thought had been cruel. The pain I held in my heart was the worst I had ever felt before. Nothing could ease it.

Sliding my feet off the bed, I sat wondering why I even got up. But my aching body needed to move. Slowly making my way to the bathroom, I stood gazing in the mirror at the face looking back at me. My eyes were almost black from lack of sleep and many hours of crying.

Taking a cold rag, I wiped my face, trying to keep from crying again. I didn't want to let my grandchildren see me upset.

Walking out of the bathroom, back into the basement where I lived, I saw the stairs that led to the main level of the house where my daughter and grandchildren lived. The stairs seemed so long. Holding on to the rail, I made my way up, one...two...three...stop. One...two...three...stop. One...two...three.... I sat on the top step as tears rolled down my face.

The door handle moved as the door opened. My five-year-old grandson Kaiden stood there looking down at me. "You okay, Grandma?"

I wiped the tears off my face. "I'm fine."

He sat down beside me and gave me a hug and kiss. Taking my hand, he stared up at me. "You miss Grandpa, don't you?"

"Yes, sweetie, I miss Grandpa."

Kaiden stood up still holding my hand, so he could help pull me up. He gave me another hug then raced to the breakfast table.

Grabbing a glass of iced tea, I stood looking out the patio door. The sun was shining, the birds were singing. Life kept on going. The world was still turning.

And the pain was still there.

When I turned back, someone had cleaned off the table, breakfast was over. I sat down and tried to read a magazine. It was hard to focus on anything. I debated about taking a walk, but I just sat there.

The sound of children playing in the living room echoed in the house and drew me to observe them. The boys were playing superheroes, while Annabelle sat watching them and laughing. Probably wondering if she should get up and play too. I'm sure she didn't know what superheroes were, being only eighteen months old. But the boys loved to make her laugh.

The sound of laughter touched my heart, yet it was hard to let go. I wondered if this hurt would ever go away, would things be normal again? I knew things could get better, but it would be without my husband by my side. I sat at the table wiping the few tears that had flowed down my cheeks.

Just then Kaiden jumped on the table in front of me, turning his bottom round and round in a circle, laughing. Stopping as fast as he started, he put his head down, making eye contact with me. I will never forget the words he said to me, words that made me smile and laugh as I hugged him tight. Words that made me realize my life was only starting a new chapter.

"If I was a superhero, Grandma, I'd fly up to Heaven and bring Grandpa back for you!"

The love of a child can make you smile.

The love of a child can make you laugh.

The love of a child will help you carry on through hard times.

The love of a child will fill your heart with love.

The love of a child sees no end.

The love of a child will always be there.

Reach out and let your heart feel the love of a child.

## IT'S NOT ALL ABOUT THE OUTSIDE

Starla Criser

My name is Harold. Would you have guessed that? Or I had a name? I'm a Ferocactus, which sounds ominous and unfriendly, I know. If you see me as a barrel cactus instead, it's not as intimidating. Right?

I'm in what they would consider my middle years, being 30. Although I could live from 50 to 130 years. 130 years sounds like forever, doesn't it? I'm not sure about that. But the alternative is scary.

I'm having what you humans call a mid-life crisis. I wanted something different to happen in my life. I got pretty bored with the same old, same old life in the Mojave Desert, in Death Valley. They don't call it the hottest place in North America for nothing. Even I sweat a little when it's 120°F from June to August. Whew! Just considering it, makes me want to happy dance about not living there any longer.

Back to that mid-life crisis thing. I got my "something different to happen in my life." I was minding my business, soaking up the sunshine, thinking even a drop or two of rain would be mighty nice. I was getting thirsty. Suddenly a Jeep came bouncing across the desert floor. The driver appeared headed for a handsome Saguaro about fifty feet from me. Tyler was one of my long-time friends. Oh, the hours we'd spent talking about things.

Sorry, I digress from telling you what happened.

I saw Tyler trying to puff up some more, trying to show his fierceness. He was a dozen feet tall and broad, too. But his size didn't keep crazy, brazen teenagers joy-riding in the desert from taking pot-shots at him from time to time. Why they thought it was hilarious to shoot holes into a helpless cactus, neither of us ever understood. And Tyler complained about it after they drove away.

Anyway, the driver veered away from Tyler and parked near me. Few people looked at me. I'm plump, about three feet wide, and I'm six feet tall. Besides that, I have ten-inch-long spines along my ribs, scarlet red ones. Ooo, scary, right?

The driver, a twentyish girl, climbed out of the Jeep, her blue-eyed gaze focused on me. She walked all around me, looking from every angle. Her long, blonde ponytail bounced behind her, and she smiled. Such a pretty smile. Admiring, innocent, curious. Then she stopped on my best side. Yes, I have a "best side." She grinned and announced, "You're perfect!"

She whipped out her cell phone and snapped some pictures. A few minutes later she and her Jeep had left. Both Tyler and I breathed easier. We laughed about the strange visit the rest of the day.

But she came back, with a big, fancy pickup truck and two guys. They took one look at me and tried to change her mind about whatever she was planning. "It's kind of big, don't you think? Maybe find another one that's smaller." "It's probably old, because of its size." "What about those spines? Are they softening, falling off?"

Their unflattering descriptions annoyed me even if they were correct. I tried to stretch my spines out as far as they would go. I'd show them!

She shook her head and said, "This one is exactly what I want."

Want? It confused me. Okay, oblivious to the idea that anything could happen to me. I'd lived here since I was a tiny seed. I'd be here until I went to cactus heaven.

I thought.

Now I'm adjusting to a significant change in my life. They dug me up although I fought against it the best I could. Those guys ended up with some serious scratches from my spines. But they were every bit as determined as the girl, trying to impress her with their machoness for nefarious reasons.

I'm living in a special spot in my girl's—Carly—backyard in Sacramento. She's got a great yard, with all kinds of trees and shrubs, many different feathery grasses, two tall and proud palms, and even some impressive canna lilies. None of them looked excited to welcome me into their world. For sure, none of them wanted me planted anywhere near them. They weren't being snobbish. I can look intimidating. They judged me on sight, on my appearance.

Since I have a spot all to myself and no longer seem threatening to them, they accept me. They've realized just because my outsides are prickly doesn't mean I have a prickly personality. I've made more than a few of them chuckle with my tales of desert life.

But I miss Tyler. If only there I could communicate with Carly. I wish I could get her to understand that my big Saguaro friend could use a good home, too. I'd even share my private garden space with him.

## THE MASTER CHEF

Bonnie Creekmore

One day the Master Chef declared,
"I'm going to make a salad,
A crispy, fine, and tasty dish,
To tempt the weak and pallid."
He chopped and tossed
With art dexterous,
And added seasonings
Quite mysterious.
Until at last—to his dismay—
He heard a voice most clamorous,
And then another and another,
In tones far less than amorous.
"I am the best! I told you so,
My color is much brighter!"
"Oh, no, you're not! I am the best,
My flavor is much lighter."
So the tomato, in his pride,
Kept his manner naughty,
And the lettuce leaf fair wilted.
They were all so naughty.
The onion smote his breast and
Declared so bold, "I'm strongest!"
The celery then stiffened his neck

And countered, "But I'm the longest."
The cauliflower began to cry,
"No one will notice me!
I'm so ugly and so bland—
Why does this have to be?"
"Without me you would all be flat,"
The salt said. Then the pepper
Stirred up a sneeze and said,
"You treat me like a leper!"
"It is enough," the Master sighed,
"What I have heard is ample.
Be still and wait until I do
My work, and then I'll sample.
He deftly stirred and tossed them all
With oil so fine and pure,
Until at last their tone had changed
To one now quite demure.
Though each had kept his character
Very well intact,
The oil had blended all of them—
Not causing to detract
From texture, form, or flavor,
Yet made them all in one,
A salad fit for any King.
The Master's work was done.

## GOOD MORNING

### Don Boldea

As morning broke free from the dark.

The birds began to sing their Good Morning melodies...

Sweet and fresh and clean.

A breeze caressed the leave of all the trees...

While the flowers opened their eyes of beauty for all

The world to see.

Oh Lord, such a way to introduce the day.

It's comforting to feel the warmth and see the light of

Another sun on the rise.

If only this Good Morning exhilaration could last for

Just a few more moments.

## CARNIVAL SUMMER CAMP

Theresa L Reiter

Through the years, my family has jokingly referred to working during the summer on the family's carnival as "attending carnival summer camp." They established the summer camp in the 1950s and it continues yet today. I attended camp from the late 1960s to the mid-1980s. It wasn't just me. Every summer, my family and extended family circle were carnies too! Since my dad was a teacher, and I was educated as a school librarian, working on the carnival added extra income for the family

I remember that during the 1960s, we all met at the Wapello County Fair lot in Eldon, Iowa to work. A week before the start of the fair, we would arrive with our tents, card tables, food and drink coolers, portable grills, and electric skillets to set up camp.

Our campsite was always in the same place—a shady strip of land next to the big lake on the fair lot. We had enough room to park cars and (this is important) it was next to a restroom. They warned us kids to stay away from the lake because cottonmouth snakes and snapping turtles inhabited the greenish water.

There would be six to ten tents of various sizes pitched next to station wagons or sedans. They used all for sleeping. Card tables, picnic tables, and lawn chairs were placed in front of the sleeping areas to ward off trespassers. They cooked and ate most meals at the campsite. Once Uncle Art caught a snapping turtle, and we enjoyed turtle soup for supper. For a special treat they allowed us to eat pancakes at a church sponsored food stand.

There was always an adult or two (usually Aunt Edith and Uncle Louie) at the campsite, plus many children—all siblings or cousins. Safety was always important, but in those days, no one worried about predators, thieves, kidnappers or pedophiles. I always felt safe, because I knew an adult was nearby.

You might ask, just what did we do at the fair?

During that time period, my parents owned a snow cone and cotton candy stand in a prime location right in front of the grandstand. The stand was a four-sided wood square covered by a canvas roof. It opened to customers from the front. My dad had built the stand and had hand-painted clowns holding our products on each side. In those days, many similar wooden structures dotted the fair lot to sell foods or provide games to fairgoers.

My dad would bring in blocks of ice to grind for the snow cones. To keep the ice blocks cold, a tarp covered them. Straw then covered the tarp. They chipped blocks of finger-numbing cold ice down to size to fit in the grinder as needed.

My mom would spin the sweet snow-white crystals while my dad would pour multi-flavored syrups over crushed ice. You can't imagine the many pounds of sugar used to make the cone syrup and to spin for the cotton candy. My sister, Tina, and cousin, Butch, sold the confections during grandstand performances as a summer job. Snow cones sold for ten cents and cotton candy on a stick for twenty-five cents.

My grandmother and uncles, Steve and Art, were the matron and Maître d's of the public restrooms close to our camp. Back then, there was no nicely furnished restrooms or even port-a-potties. Grandma and the uncles provided toilet paper, paper towels, and soap for the restrooms. Grandma also supplied feminine supplies for the women and the uncles put out bowls, shaving cream and razors for the men. They paid for these items out of their own pockets. Their mode of income (and pay-back) from this venture was the tips they gleaned from the patrons. My job was to assist my grandma when she needed a break or to replenish supplies. I remember seeing many fair folk washing or shaving daily using these items. One summer, my goal was to earn enough money to purchase the latest LP by the teen rock group, The Monkees. I earned $5.98 to buy it!

Silly as it sounds, we girls would have a great time in these restrooms! Imagine a high wooden partition with a row of fifteen toilet seat holes on each side. There were no flushing handles, but gushes of running water in a trench under the seats that started in the women's restroom and continued through the men's facility. We would drop sticks, rocks, or small objects down the first hole and watch it travel down the stream of water. We never went in the men's side, so we never knew where our items would end up! I doubt those restrooms are there now!

Aunt Cecile and Aunt Ethel had a booth under the grandstand where they sold handmade items. Fairgoers could inspect hand sewn aprons, placemats, tablecloths, crocheted doilies, sock monkeys and such that they had for sale. They even entered the open fair classes in sewing and won some ribbons! All the vendor booths under the grandstand had sawdust covered floors.

Often my Aunt Mary Margaret or Uncle Jerry ran a game or a ride for the carnival or helped to set up and tear down to earn money.

When we kids were not working they allowed us to travel the fair lot. We visited the animal barns, 'judged' livestock competitions, toured exhibit buildings, watched grandstand performances through a broken fence, or just 'hung around.' Sometimes the 4-H kids would let us pet their animals or sit on their ponies. To the dismay of our parents we always went home with many free items from the businesses.

When the fair was over, the stand taken down, everything packed, money counted, and people paid, we would meet at the local restaurant to eat before leaving for home. Later that restaurant became owned by Rosanne Barr and Tom Arnold.

The purpose of carnival summer camp was to build character and responsible traits. And earn money! I think myself and my children are more assertive and confident from their stint at camp.

Those were the glory days. Maybe a strange way to spend a week in the summer, but one we'll always remember!

# FOREVER HOME

## Jan Koelsch

My name is Violet. I am a stray dog. Some people call me a mutt. I don't have a home. Today it is freezing. Ice is coming down from the sky. My nose is cold! It is just too cold for a little dog like me. I wish my fur was thicker and my ears longer. I know I need a forever home where it is warm, safe and comfy.

My lizard friend, Tumbleweed said he had a forever home once. He felt safe there. He always had food. The guy that took him from the pet store was good to him. Then a cat came to live with them. Tumbleweed said the cat thought Tumbleweed was a toy.

"I became scared of the cat," Tumbleweed said, with a faraway look in his eye.

One day after the cat batted him around a lot, Tumbleweed decided to run away from his home. The cat was asleep. An open window was a way to escape. Tumbleweed slipped by the cat out the window. He said he didn't believe in a forever home.

I believe there is a forever home somewhere just for me. I hope to find one this very day.

I trotted over to the grocery store. The butcher would sometimes leave a bone for me at the back door. Today he met me there with a big, juicy hambone with tiny pieces of meat. Yummy!

As soon as I finished the bone, the butcher said it was time for me to go. He booted me out the door. Said dogs weren't supposed to be inside.

The grade school just up the street was my next stop. Kids go to school. Sometimes they take dogs like me home. One little girl noticed me shivering. She took me inside the school. Her hugs were warming me. The icicles had melted off my ears.

Other kids ventured over to see how they could help. We were having a great time until a big man called the principal heard the kids laughing.

"What's this?" the principal said gruffly, as he looked down at me.

The little girl looked at him with big sad eyes.

"This poor dog was outside. He was shaking. We are just trying to get him warm."

"Children, you need to go to your classrooms right NOW! I'll take care of the dog."

The little girl patted me on the head. "I hope you get a warm place to stay," she whispered in my ear. "I wish it could be home with me." Then she left.

"As for you, dog," the principal snarled as he opened the door, "OUT! This is NOT your home!" He slammed the door behind me. The door just missed my tail.

The sleet had stopped. It was time to find a place to sleep. I never knew about the weather. I looked around and noticed the park across the street. A picnic table was there. Someone had left a bit of food. Some blew to the ground.

I ran across the street. A car just missed hitting me. Boy! Was that close! Never a dull moment looking for a forever home. This might be a good place for now. It wasn't my forever home though.

Kids talking loudly as they got off the bus woke me up the next morning. The warm sun made everything better today. I stretched and shook myself as I glanced around. An older man sat on the park bench with something warm in his hand. Steam circled in the air.

"Maybe he will share with me," I thought. "He looks sad. He might know where there are forever homes for a dog like me." I was cute and little with pretty eyes.

I slowly walked over to the park bench. I lay down and just happened to rest my head on the older man's foot. The man looked down and smiled.

"Well, who is this?"

My tail wagged as I kept my head on his foot. The man bent down and patted my head.

As he pulled a sandwich out of his pocket, he asked, "Are you hungry?" He laid half the sandwich on the ground right under my nose. There was no way I would leave that sandwich there. As I gobbled it up, I heard the man chuckle. "Oh, my! You are a hungry dog. Here, eat this, too." Right in front of me was the other half sandwich. Wow! This was great!

"My name is Tim. How would you like to come to my house? I am looking for a new friend. You are just a perfect little girl."

Was this Tim serious? Did he really want me to go to his house?

Tim stood up. "Come on. Let's go home, little girl."

My name is not 'little girl,' but Tim had said the word home. I jumped up as high as my legs could—right into Tim's arms. That caught him by surprise and almost knocked him off his feet.

Tim laughed and pulled me close. I snuggled up against him. He began walking. "Little girl, see that house on the corner. That is your new home. You are home with me forever."

Tim was right. I was home—forever.

## THERE YOU STOOD UPON THE BRIDGE
### Martha Williams Prentice

There you stood upon the bridge,
    your form reflected in the stream,

or was it recall from a dream
    wind-swept on yonder ridge.

Return to me, so I can breathe,
    and fill this cold and dreaded space

where once my heart kissed your embrace.
    Come back, my life bequeath.

## YOUR EYES

Coe Holden

Your eyes are like stars, your cheeks like a rose.

The sunlight in your hair could melt a thousand snows.

Music is love looking for a word.

May your hands always be stretched out in friendship and never in want.

Good friends are good for your health.

Other things may change us, but we start and end with love.

## ON THE STAGE

Coe Holden

I came to town with my Guitar on my back.

I went to the Saloon to sing for a snack.

Then owner said I should be on stage,

The next stage out of town.

## MY THREE PETS:

### A Memoir of Unconditional Love

E. L. Morrow

I consider myself fortunate to have bonded with three non-human creatures. Each one came to me at the time I needed them even though I didn't understand my need until later. There have been other animals in my life, or my home but none of them developed the unexplainable connection sometimes experienced across species lines—at least not with me.

You see, I believe these pets choose me. We humans believe we're "in charge" of everything. But from time to time we learn lessons from those more in-touch with some grounded-rooted-instinctive truths. Pets can ground us—and remind us why we need reality as our foundation.

It is still true that we humans may be the ones who go to the pet store or take in the stray. But who is to say that we are not led to that decision by some yet undetermined need? The need may be as simple as wanting something else to pick up after, or to expand the horizons for a child in our care.

But, sometimes the relationship moves beyond "interesting creature that does tricks," to "dependable companion who gives insights." When it happens, the pet creates and nurtures the change. It is a small action of the same spirit that orders the universe, stepping in and adjusting one aspect of life through an inner-species exchange.

I'm beginning to sound like a preacher. Well, old habits die hard. But back to the story of the attempts of three animals to improve the life of one different from themselves.

******

Before I can talk about the impact of my three pets, I need to say a few words about my first pet—the one I never received.

My mother had three older brothers. In her family, when a boy reached a certain age, they received a dog. She said, "Every boy should have a dog." In my father's family dogs were tolerated because they kept the chickens safe. My mother thought I should have a small dog to live in the house. My daddy said, "Never! Outside in the garage." I wasn't sure if he meant that I should move to the garage with the dog, or me in the house, but dog outside.

My Uncle Charlie, one of mother's brothers-in-law, worked on the railroad as a switchman. People would come to the switchyard to leave unwanted animals—mostly dogs and cats. Though he did mention an alligator, and a box full of turtles. Uncle Charlie was soft-hearted and couldn't allow any animal to suffer. So, he brought home most of the animals (not the alligator).

Fortunately, they lived on a tract of fifty aches all wooded land except where they built their home and a large pen for the dogs. A creek ran through it, plus a freshwater spring supplied the drinking water.

My mother and aunt had been talking about my "need for a dog," when Uncle Charlie picked up a small dog, about six months old. The description convinced my mother that this puppy was what I needed. One problem: we lived in Orlando, Florida, and the dog was in Charlotte, North Carolina. We learned about the dog just before Christmas, but it would be next summer before we could make a trip to collect this creature. Mother figured it would take that long to convince my father that I could be responsible enough to care for the dog. From the description of the animal, brown and white, I gave him a very original name: Brownie.

About a month before the trip to bring home my first pet, Brownie got hit by a car.

I learned from my first-non-pet: things don't always go as planned.

******

My actual first pet was a duck. My father believed everything should be practical. The "sanitation code" prohibited chickens where we lived. Back in those days, you could buy "chicks" and "baby ducklings" some of them their natural color, and some dyed like Easter eggs. When I was ten, my dad purchased three "baby ducks" before Easter. A box in the dining room provided their first home.

Something happened to the others, and we soon had only one. I gave her another original name: Duckie.

As she grew, Dad built a pen outside. My bedroom being closest to both the enclosure and the back door, it became my job to listen for any threat during the night. I also had the task of letting her out in the morning, providing her food and when she started laying—collecting her egg. Duckie provided one egg per day for almost three years.

My mother and four-year-old sister went to "the shop." My dad, a self-employed roofer, kept materials, tools and an office there. My mother answered the phone did the bookkeeping, invoices, mail and that sort of stuff. So, no one would be home when I returned from school.

I walked to and from school each day, about eight blocks. When I returned home, Duckie would come down the driveway from the backyard to greet me. Usually, she would not venture out of our backyard or the neighbor's. Our duck kept both yards free of bugs. She knew what time I should be coming from school, so she greeted me. I would sit on the back steps; she would hop into my lap and put her long neck up to and sometimes over my shoulder. Then she would "nibble" on my hair, making a low quacking sound. I decided that was her version of a cat's purring. I would stroke her from head to tail. The feathers on her head and neck were soft and the others silky smooth. We had this daily ritual.

I have to tell you, like the rest of her family, Duckie had some quirks. For example, she would not swim. We had a big old-style washtub of water, large enough for a duck to swim. She would walk over to it and drink water. I picked her up one day and placed her in the water.

She got out so fast and with such determination that she soaked me in the process. She quickly waddled away, dried herself and wouldn't have anything to do with me as long as I stood near the water.

Duckie would clean herself by taking her head and "rolling" a few drops of water on her back. Next, she would use her bill to strip and groom each feather. It would take her about an hour each time, and she did this every day.

After a while neighbors complained about the "wild animal" we harbored. An acquaintance from church agreed to take her. They had ducks and a lake. After they took her, we learned she slept under the house with the dogs. She wanted nothing to do with those funny white creatures that got in the water.

From my duck, I learned how pleasant it is to touch and be touched by another living creature. My family was not demonstrative. We only touched if required: checking for a fever, applying a body rub, things like that. But this duck wanted me to hold and pet her for no reason—it seemed to make her feel safe. That was another first for me—being a protector.

I also learned that animals could talk to us if we will listen. Duckie made different sounds when nibbling my hair or shoelaces, when spotting danger (a snake), or when afraid (when a dog caught her by the tail feathers).

******

My next pet did not come for more than forty years. While my children had the usual stream of goldfish, aquarium fish, parakeets, and a couple of dogs. None of them bonded with me, or for that matter the kids either. Bonding with a fish is hard. My sister learned that lesson at the age of two. She would take her goldfish out and stroke it, very gently with one finger. When the fish became really calm, she would put it back in the water. Amazingly, many times it would swim around.

Back to my second pet. My wife and I attended a luncheon meeting at the home of a colleague. While getting the tour of the house, a calico cat ran out from behind a couch heading for a door to the garage. I said, "What a beautiful cat!" She turned around, came back to let me pet her until a slight noise sent her dashing away.

After dinner we talked about their animals: they had two dogs, and three more cats, probably a hamster in one of the children's rooms. I mentioned the beautiful calico cat. Our host said, "Oh, you saw the invisible cat? Would you like her?"

I thought she was joking. Why would anyone give away such a gorgeous, friendly animal? We asked, "what's wrong with her."

We learned: the cat is miserable; lives behind the couch except to run to the litter box and back again. The dogs and other cats torment her, and the children ignore her. So, we ended up getting the cat the next afternoon. She cried all the way to our house, about three miles.

We let her out in our bedroom, thinking she could get used to the upstairs where we had her litter box and feeding station. She ran immediately under the bed and stayed. After our coaxing failed, we left her to explore on her own. I worked on something on the computer downstairs. Quiet prevailed, no radio or TV. After examining the upstairs, she came downstairs. She checked out every available space learning no other four-legged types were living in this house. When she found me, she hopped into my lap. From that moment on, she became my cat.

We named her Ginger. She was about four-years-old when she came to us. Ginger filled my life with joy, companionship, and lessons for fourteen more years.

Sometimes we referred to her as the miracle cat. Before our friends received this cat, a church member that lived out "in the country" asked if they would take her. It seems a farmer couldn't give away a batch of kittens. He took a sack full of kittens out in the cornfield and shot the bag with a shotgun blast. He dumped them out on the ground. All dead, except one—playing dead. When he turned to walk away, the survivor ran in the opposite direction. The farmer later called his neighbors to say that a little kitten might wander on their property and why.

They found the kitten. Thought of their pastor who had just lost a pet, and the rest is history.

Ginger came to us at a time when our work brought extreme stress. My wife and I worked with a troubled and troubling organization. A fair percentage of the people we worked with displayed hostility, manipulation, or resentfulness. Some said we had been sent to "fix them." We perceived our jobs as empowering them, helping the healing to begin, and looking toward a more productive and faithful future.

To the degree that any of our goals occurred, a four-legged-calico-cat is partially responsible. She helped us de-stress while providing nonjudgmental acceptance. She spoke plainly about her few needs: food, clean water, litter that does not smell and a place to hide. What she wanted; however, was for us to sit down on a couch, or chair and to let her join us. It didn't work if we picked her up and put her in our laps, or between us. She would tolerate that until she could get away. She would usually come back, when it was her idea, and then we would pet or brush her while she serenaded us with her purring.

From Ginger, I relearned the importance of taking time to be with those we love.

I also learned it is important to talk to your pets and explain things. Part of the time, I worked three hours away and had an apartment there. I would spend from four to six days per week there, and the remainder in Wichita. I took Ginger to be with me as a companion. She still hated to travel, so I would leave her in the apartment unless I would be away for more than three days. Before leaving, I would tell her how many nights I would be gone. I would then count out the number by holding her tail between "flops" equal to the number of nights.

I thought the counting of nights was just a ritual performed for my benefit until one time when I was delayed an extra two days. Ginger gave me the cold shoulder for a whole day.

Ginger also had strong opinions about loyalty. Sometime in my work, I would encounter other's pets, and they would rub against my legs or shoes. The moment I returned Ginger would sniff my feet and then hiss at me. She liked being the only pet. My having been with another animal meant I might bring another animal into our space. I think the hissing was a protest to any other animals being added to our household.

******

While I was working out of town several days a week, we got a dog to keep my wife company. She had fallen in love with the Corgi breed while some church members trained them as therapy dogs. While getting groceries, we saw a sign about Corgi puppies and called the phone number. We called and found only one remained, so we went to see it—and he came home with us.

My wife named him Phoenix since two of our children lived in a city by that name. We later learned that he was a "throw-back." He had some of the genetic traits of an intermediary stage in the development of the final version of the breed. That made him slightly taller, longer and heavier than the breed standard. It also meant that he had a particularly compassionate, loyal, and determined personality.

He kept her company when I was away. He saw his job as protecting my wife, me, and the cats who lived under our roof. Bringing joy and playing jokes were also part of his responsibility.

When Phoenix first came into our home, we already had two cats: Ginger, and Maggie. The latter had been my mother-in-law's. Until we knew how they would get along, we declared the upstairs for the cats, and downstairs for the dog.

The dog would start upstairs, and we would call him back. The landing at the bottom of the stairs could be entered from two sides. The living room or an overgrown stairwell being used as a home office. The puppy started up the stairs, we called, and he did not come. So, we went to get him, but he wasn't on the stairs. We had a gate at the top of the stairs to keep him out. Could he possibly have jumped the barrier? We went upstairs and checked—no Phoenix. We came downstairs wondering, and he came out from behind the couch—he bounced up and down and making a kind of chuckle noise. He was laughing. He had played a joke on us. He went through the stairwell around the corner and behind the sofa while we were looking for him upstairs. And he waited until we came down to pull his coup d'état.

We never again had to tell him not to go upstairs. Soon the cats came down and found him to be tolerable. Both cats came to like the dog, better than each other.

One of the things I learned from Phoenix is that courage has little to do with size. When only six months old, my wife took him for a walk when a full-grown pit-bull charged them. This puppy raised up on his hind legs, lifted his front paws above his head and made a sound similar to a lion. The other dog stopped and backed away. The other dog's owner came running, "What did you do to my dog?" My wife responded, "Nothing. But there is a leash law here."

I need to say a little about Maggie. She had been a stray showing up on my wife's mom's doorstep one cold December night. Since she lived next door, she became our cat as well. Maggie was about two when the puppy arrived. She tried to teach him how to be a cat.

Maggie would see him using the backyard as a toilet, so, she got his attention, dug a hole in soft dirt, and stepped away. Phoenix sniffed the hole and went to a tree to relieve himself. The cat tried again, digging the hole deeper, and sitting over it to demonstrate the proper use of a hole. The dog again sniffed the hole and pooped in the yard.

I could sense the cat's frustrations was beyond words—meows for her. So, she used the hole, covered it up and walked away with an air of superiority that only a cat can carry off.

About that time the dog and cat played hide and seek. Maggie would hide under or behind a piece of furniture, and the dog would run around the room. As he ran around the room, the cat would reach out and tag him on his rear, and retreat. The next time the dog would turn back in time to lick the cat on her nose. He would be so happy after kissing the cat.

Maggie started taking walks with us. When we would take the dog on a leash, and the cat would follow along, or run a house or two ahead. Phoenix and I walked on the sidewalk or at the curb; Maggie would walk closer to the homes where she could get to shrubs or under vehicles.

The neighborhood where we walked had little traffic. People would see one of us walking the dog and stop to ask, "Where's the cat?" We would point her out. Everyone thought it was so strange.

If for any reason the cat slowed down or was frightened by something she would stop and so would Phoenix. If Maggie could not resolve the issue on her own, we would go back. Often the cat would run and catch up with us; sometimes we would change the route of our walk--it was always the dog that decided—I trusted his nose far better than mine.

I learned that dogs understand more about symbolism than we might think. The dog, cat and I walked one evening. On a street not frequently traveled by us, Maggie was two houses ahead. A male cat, larger and fiercer came from across the street to confront our cat. Phoenix was ready to rush in and save his "sister," but I said, "no, she's got to face him down, or he'll find her some other time." They hissed, growled and snarled, but never got close enough to hurt each other. They went to a crouching position ready to pounce, about three feet apart. After several minutes the male blinked first and got up and trotted to a safe distance but lingered close-by.

You know the saying that dogs have owners and cats have a staff. Maggie got up and came close to us, sort of saying to the other cat, "I've got a better 'staff' than you." Meanwhile, Phoenix went to the depression in the grass made by the male and urinated all over it. He stopped to look at the male cat and gave out a low single "woof." Translation: "You mess with my sister, you'll answer to me."

A popular saying is, "No good deed goes unpunished." In K-9 justice all good deeds are rewarded. One time Phoenix had something caught in his throat. Each gasp seemed more labored. After more than enough time for him to clear it, I used a finger to dislodge it. Starting then, I had a dog. He never abandoned my wife, but he never wanted to be far from me.

He traveled with us to Niagara Falls, Brookland, Boston, Virginia, Tennessee, Arizona. Plus, numerous trips to Oklahoma, Missouri, Illinois, and parts of Kansas. He stayed close to me, anytime he could, including during my writing. No more than two feet away while I wrote and revised The Doorkeeper's Secrets and the first drafts of the next novel, The Doorkeeper's Mind.

I learned about loyalty from this Corgi. He was with me when I fell and broke a bone in my hand. When a dog attacked us, he drew the attention away from me, till the other dog's owners got their animal under control. He sensed danger from an angry man a block away on a crowded street—where we needed to pass. Phoenix refused to budge from the corner until the angry man stomped away—then we walked down the block. He loved walks, children, balls to catch, our cats, us, and food.

I don't know if he would have behaved differently with a different family, but he functioned as an introvert. He was quiet and calm. Told us when he needed something and waited patiently (most of the time) for our response. He was protective and appreciative of all we did for him.

One final lesson from him is about dying. Rituals are important to dogs as well as people. One of our routines was a trip outside before bed. Most nights it involved a walk, at least a block. The walks for his last week had been only a few houses. On what would be his last night, he did not leave our yard. He sat in the cool grass for about 20 minutes. I now realize he may have been surveying and remembering all the changes in his home.

The next morning it became clear it was time. We called the vet who comes to the house for such times. But Phoenix took care of that as well. He refused to eat, only drank a couple sips of water. He was surrounded by our two cats, our younger Corgi and us. We each had our time to say our farewells. Even the cat who never liked either of the dogs sat three feet away quietly watching (with what we interpreted as respect).

Saying goodbye is difficult. Writing these words has been hard but also a bit freeing. The memories of one creature's unconditional love for another helps us get back to a degree of equilibrium. Later in the day, my wife said it best, "We seem smaller—as a family." It feels like we are diminished—shrunken by an absence.

*******

We still have two cats, one Corgi and two adults in our family. None of the non-human ones have the personality of those mentioned earlier. I don't expect to ever bond with another animal like I have these three unique pets. If it happens, it will be a gift.

Winston, our younger Corgi, brought joy and energy to Phoenix in his last years. In his last week, they played, tussled, and wrestled until the older dog ran out of energy.

Winston has taken up the mantle of being the household protector. He also realized that I had a big hole in my life when Phoenix left us, so he spends a lot of time near me. Still going to bed as soon as it gets dark, but Winston and I have started taking a walk shortly before I turn in for the evening. He's smart, gentle and respectful. While he is not a "replacement" for our loss—he is unique and is contributing to our sense of well-being.

Talking about grief is essential. Healing begins when we remember what we have learned and treasured from the missing one. To look forward to tomorrow, with the gift from the past, and loves from today is the best most of us can achieve.


My tomorrow is a brighter day because of my three pets, their companions, plus the friends and pets of today. My wish for each person is that you find the unconditional love I found from human and non-human sources. If you do, you will have a blessed today and tomorrow.

# HARRY'S DATE

## Gwendolyn Eldridge Gandy

Harry called yesterday to ask if I would be free to join him for dinner and dancing tonight. It thrilled me, Susan Miller, to be asked. So, of course, I said yes.

I had been waiting for over a week and doing whatever I could at our bridge club to get him to notice me. I asked him to hang on the phone while I checked my calendar to make sure I hadn't already made other plans. I knew nothing else was on my calendar, but a lady shouldn't appear too anxious. Shortly I returned to the telephone and told him I was free to go with him.

He was a little confused because he had asked me the same question yesterday but didn't remember. I told Harry to please put the phone close to his ear and repeated loudly the day (Saturday) and the time (6:00 pm) that we had already on. "Harry, write it down so you don't forget."

He said he would. Here at Sunny Grove Retirement Home, we have rules about everyone being in their room by 9:30 pm and lights out no later than 10:30 pm, every night.

All day long I had been searching through my closet trying to find something to wear on my evening out with Harry. My friend Helen came over to help me decide on a dress.

"Helen, what do you think of this black one?" I asked as I stood in front of the mirror looking at myself.

"I don't like it," she said, shaking her head. "Well, it is a little daring, cut too low in the front for a woman in her nineties. Let's see you in the navy blue one."

I slip it on and we both thought it was way too short. My knees showed.

"Don't even put on that pink flower one. You will just look like a walking flower pot," Helen said.

So I grabbed the white dress. It was a good fit and flattered my small waist line.

Men are different. They don't worry about what they are going to wear, just put on a suit and they are good to go. Harry had picked up his on sale at a men's store that was going out of business.

Harry arrived at my door even though he had to walk through the fog from his apartment to Sunny Grove which is next door. When he knocked at my door, it was 6 o'clock. I took my time going to answer the door because I couldn't walk any faster.

When I opened the door, Harry looked great in his white tux with a lime green cummerbund and holding red flowers. He bowed and took my hand, kissed me on the cheek, and then I smiled.

We waddled the hallway together for our dinner and dance. We had thirty minutes to find the cafeteria for an evening of fun.

# DOCTOR TRIP
## Susan Howell

My car, Henrietta, waits for me patiently
as I take my time, doing what I need.
Then, she takes charge, awakening
with a soft hum, recognizing I am here.

Slowly, together, she backs us up
until we both are startled by a crunch,
and the sound of her antenna rolling,
along the echoing garage floor.

The garage door, the villain,
slowly rises, looking innocent.

The damage is major, her electronics,
wires and broken screws exposed
to the ravages of the elements.
Whatever is needed to fix her, I must do.

Today we will go to her family physician,

Doctor Scholfield, for the diagnosis.

Will her entire assembly need to be replaced?

Or, can some squirts of gorilla glue do the trick?

Of course, this is the doctor's world

where gorilla glue is not allowed.

Only entirely new parts at three times

original cost grace the shelves of this clinic.

Yet, she also needs new oil to loosen her limbs

and new coolant to comfort mine.

So a trip to the doctor was still in order

even though I wasn't ready to take her this time.

I wonder if she and the garage door were in cahoots

to set up this trip and the need for this fix.

You never know with supposedly inanimate objects

What goes on in their minds, their bag of tricks.

## THE DUST BOWL IN KANSAS

Mabel Helen Braddy

(via Joan Morrison)

I, Mabel Helen Braddy, was born in Stanton County, Johnson City, Kansas close to the Colorado border May 5, 1932 to James Otis and Arlene Helen Ford. These were the Dust Bowl years.

When I was about six my family and another family went to the state of Washington to look for work. Dad had a truck which we used as living quarters. The two families traveled together.

We found work at Chelan, Washington picking apples (Red Delicious apples). Chelan is in the middle of the state in the Wenatchee National Forest on the Columbia River in the mountains. We lived in a cabin at the edge of the apple orchard. I started first grade there. We rode a bus to school, crossing the Columbia River to and from school. The school was at the top of a mountain.

When harvest was finished that year in the fall, we left Chelan and went to Idaho where we had relatives living there. I began school again there in first grade. We didn't live there long when Grandfather Ford died back in Johnson City, Kansas. So, Dad, Mother and I and an aunt went back, and I began school again—he third time—before Thanksgiving.

Sometime during the early years of my life—1932 to about 1936 or 1937—we noticed a black sky to the west. It looked like a black cloud with heavy wind. Mom and I had to get the chickens into the barn to keep them from blowing away.

It was blowing soil. There was no farming. The dust was blowing everywhere. Mom put sheets over the windows to keep the dust out. At meal time we had to keep the lids on the pans to keep dust out and even then food would be a little gritty.

A neighbor took his children to school and would stop for me every Monday morning. I took the equivalent of a three-pound coffee can full of fresh eggs. When I got to school, I took them up to the lunch room and paid with them for my lunch for the week. These neighbors lost a child with "dust pneumonia."

Then the following year when I finished second grade, we moved again—to Ulysses, about 22 miles east of Johnson City, and Dad worked for the state highway department.

On December 25th, Christmas Day, 1940 my brother Jimmy was born. The following year, 1941, they bombed Pearl Harbor in December. Dad built a small trailer house, and we moved to Wichita where he went to work at Boeing.

# FALL COLORS

## Our McDowell Walking Group Trip

Joan Morrison

As trips go, this one has to be one of the special ones. It was intended to be a "walk in the woods to enjoy the fall colors," but it turned out to be an adventure.

To this purpose, this writer got up at 7:30 a.m. thinking, *Oh it will just be the usual walk the McDowell group takes around town, or maybe they will go to one of the parks nearby. I'll be home in an hour.* I forgot the item in the Center's bulletin said Blackhand Gorge. *As a footnote, the McDowell Senior Center is now called the Dodge Recreation Center

When I arrived at the Center and learned it was a van trip, and we would stop somewhere for lunch, I thought, *I've always wanted to see Blackhand Gorge. Pictures of tall cliffs and rugged scenery this close to Columbus (Ohio) makes it accessible and a curiosity. We'll be back by one o'clock probably.* But I hate to leave my husband without a car when he thinks I'll only be gone an hour. So, I called from the Center. He said, "It'll be ok. Enjoy yourself."

We took I-70 east to State Route 13 OK. Then north to Newark and Route 16. Well, in the pretty and interesting town of Newark we missed a sign and went the wrong way ending up at the end of the street. We circled back and stopped at a street repair truck where a workman was busy repairing the street. Carol (group staff member and driver) got out and asked directions to Route 16. Actually, if we had looked up we could see it, a highway built on viaducts carrying heavy traffic over the houses. A turn left, a right at the light, and we were on our way.

Then we drove and drove, passing several county roads, looking for

Marne or "Tabasco." We ran out of four-lane divided highway to a place where road construction crews were working. We had been on our way to Coshocton. Carol pulled over to the side and got out, hailed a construction flag lady and was told we passed the road to Blackhand Gorge.

Yes, we backtracked to CR 668 and turned left off 16. We had passed Dillon State Park on our right but decided that wasn't it.

At 668 just off the highway, we saw a school bus repair shop and turned in. We inquired of someone there about Blackhand Gorge. While there we saw a rough map on the bulletin board showing how to get to "Toboso." Up 16 to 146, turn right to 273, go a mile or two just before Toboso and you're there. The secretary was very helpful as well as a shop man. After most of us used the restroom, we went on.

So, we went that way and found it. The walk was as far as four miles one way, which Alice and I only did about one and a half miles. It was fun as all eleven of us took the wide paved path through trees between high cliffs, overlooking the Licking River in places, with high cliffs on the other side some places; under a railroad trestle, past points marking other trails through the woods. (The trestle crossed a path by an overhead railroad.) It was chilly in the shade on the walk for the most part but warm where sunny.

We met a local woman on her walk who worked at the Longaberger Basket Co.. We had passed the Longaberger Company's "basket" building along Route 16 just north of Newark. She recommended that we lunch at the Cottage Inn in Hanover, which is just the other side of Route 16 by way of 146. We saw other bikers and walkers on the trail.

We finished walking, had the regular meeting of the walkers group sitting on the steps of a log cabin by its parking lot.

Jackie pointed out the wildlife, a fuzzy gray worm with two horns at each end and eyes at one end. We enjoyed the warmth of the sun, the colorful trees, each other's company.

We got on our way. This time I was at the front passenger seat co-piloting since I remembered the woman's directions to the restaurant. But my memory just took us to the outskirts of Hanover.

We swung off to the right past some houses because we didn't want to follow Marne Road to Marne. The road took us out of town, past a park, then a sharp turn at a railroad overpass. Carol blew the horn going through. Then left out into some more town to a traffic light.

I said, "Let's stop at this station on the right and ask directions."

Someone on the bus said, "Oh look—there's Cottage Inn Restaurant." A small but attractive little place. We parked at the front door in the handicap zone and all filed out of the van.

After a fun hour or so of good food and special dessert pies, we headed out. Carol said, "Where?" I pointed south. She said, "This way—heading east?" I thought it might lead around and back to 16 so I said ok. But it is Licking Valley Road and we head northeast, clear out of the county.

So again, we find a school—a long one story neat but small and old building. Carol went in and asked—came out and said we have to go clear back to where we left the restaurant. Must have been several miles over hills and around bends past farms and barns and houses old and new, small and elaborate, fields of stacked hay.

Back at the restaurant we turned right, northwest it looked to me, and she pulled up at an ice cream parlor a block away where a semi-truck driver sat in his cab. Carol inquired about the way to get back to 16 and Columbus.

"Which part of Columbus do you want?" he said. Carol said, "I don't know—does it matter?" So, he gave her directions to take 37 south off 16 and she made a map on a scrap of paper.

We went that way, continuing on through Hanover up a hill where school kids are letting out.

At the top we could see 16 off in the distance where fast traffic was moving. On to 16 again, we got to 37, only it was 37 east and 37 west.

We decided east was wrong (but it was right because it goes south)—missed 37 west because it was obvious it went northwest and just stayed on 16.

I guided her to Pataskala on 16, then south on 310 to 70, to 4th Street. She got off because traffic was backed up on 70 at 4th St.

We got back by Front St., Town St., and McDowell and we were home—by 3:30! And me, guilty as sin, remembering I was supposed to pick up Tammy who had to call her sister.

All eleven of us enjoyed a very adventurous fun trip. How many waystanders did we seek directions from? At least five—the road paver in Newark, the lady flag bearer at the construction site, the school bus repair shop, the semi driver in Hanover, the schoolhouse secretary on Licking Valley Road. We got a good lesson in local culture. Oh yes, and the lady on the trail who recommended Cottage Inn where her son worked.

Now you may think why did the driver take off without better directions to Blackhand Gorge? But Carol, a seasoned trip leader, probably thought, that it was so close to Columbus, and she had been up in that area before, all we needed was a state map.

Flint Ridge and Dawes Arboretum are in the area and actually are not hard to find because they are near state routes. But Blackhand Gorge is reached by way of county roads, which don't show on state maps. It is a fairly new natural wildlife area open to the public and not so well known. And haven't you just gone off on a pretty day with your friends exploring, expecting to enjoy the ride for itself? And you stumble onto your destination somehow, sometimes having to inquire of locals?

Actually, inquiring of people in the area is no problem with Carol. I think she enjoys it for its own sake. She has no problem with talking to strangers, she likes it. Your typical recreation center leader—outgoing, relaxed, and with a take-things-as-they-come manner.

As for me, I'd get kind of uptight. But then think, this is my chance to unwind, don't worry, settle down and just enjoy the scenery and the people. As long as others are enjoying themselves and don't complain—and one could complain about almost anything—the trip is more pleasant for others. This was a good chance to get away from the daily grind for a change. It wasn't as if I did this often. That's the point of recreation. We can all do this more often—just take a day and let come what may.

After reading this, Carol laughed so hard as she remembered all the experiences on this trip that she said she had to run to the bathroom (not the way she said it). Not everyone is so good a sport.

Did I mention the fall colors at Blackhand Gorge and everywhere else? They were beautiful in shades of gold, yellow, orange, red, green and brown.

## VENUS RISING HIGH, SO HIGH
### Martha Williams Prentice

Venus rising high, so high
  at midnight hour in eastern sky,
this April night I contemplate
  your shining light toward Heaven's gate.

So singular your astral journey
  among the countless of ageless story
through silent space with speed unmeasured
  all synchronized, divinely treasured.

I almost think you follow me
  so I'll look up at you to see
how captive just a thought can be,
  your lovely, secret hold on me.

## WHO WE ARE!

Rochelle Boster

Who are we?

Self-made? Doubtful since we didn't spring from the ground like a weed, but rather a DNA cocktail of elders and ancestors.

Who are we?

Successful? Define it. Even the homeless person on the street has days of success when the sun is shining and the blanket warm.

Who are we?

Self-centered? You can't deny the most giving of us have moments of self-pity for how we have been mistreated, real or unreal.

Who are we?

Opinionated? Each one of us has bumped into a reason why we think, feel, and express ourselves in ways different to others. Who's right, who's wrong?

Who are we?

Judgemental? Human kind excels at judging. Accepting difference into the norm is defined as weakness and many times shunned.

WHO WE ARE is very simple. We are a basket load of relationships, experiences, emotions, opportunities. Turning right, turning left, saying yes, saying no. Who we are represents each choice we have made since the very beginning of our time. Who we are is a well stirred sometimes shaken compilation of every moment of our existence.

Celebrate who you are, because you are unique! Own the best parts of you, but don't deny the best parts of others.

## LIVING

Bonnie Lacey Krenning

Trees and grass and fields of wild flowers.
Playing and sleeping.
Mom cooking:
Eggs, milk, biscuits, molasses, gravy, cracklins, greens, mushrooms.
Brothers everywhere; pampering, disciplining and teasing.
Daddy was sick; he couldn't hold me.
The doctor came; Daddy had blood poisoning, fever.
The days were hot, and the nights.
The neighbors stood over Daddy fanning, day and night.
July, '34; Missouri, misery.

The doctor came.
My brothers said Mom was tired; she couldn't hold me.
The doctor picked me up and told me I had two new baby brothers.
I already had brothers of every size.
A baby brother, brothers about my size and big brothers like Daddy.
Hot; no rain, only hot days and nights and fussy, crying babies.
The neighbors stood over them and Mom, fanning day and night.

## Starla Criser

The doctor came; he left quietly.

The neighbors were there, quiet and unsmiling.

Grandpa said the baby had gone to Heaven to be with God.

But Daddy built a box and they put him in the ground.

The man in strange clothes said the baby's spirit was in Heaven.

I hoped my spirit didn't go to Heaven.

I was barely three.

The rains came!

We had to shoo the chickens inside so they wouldn't drown.

They didn't know what rain was.

Now the chickens would lay eggs again, the cows would give milk again.

We romped and splashed and played in the rain.

Too late, the rain, for Spring and Summer crops; they never came up.

Daddy and my brothers planted acres of turnips; they grew fast.

We ate turnips and all the animals ate turnips.

The cow's milk tasted like turnips, the sausage tasted like turnips.

Winter winds same through the wooden floors and around the doors and windows.

Mom and Daddy slept with my little brother and the baby and me.

To keep us warm, because the wood fires went out at night.

Also, to keep us protected from the rats.

Spring! Everything in the house was loaded on the wagon; we had no car.

Daddy and my big brothers were building a new home.

Made from trees they cut and sawed at the saw mill.

Just framework and boxing; he'd build a better one later.

They had to hurry and plant spring crops.

Days of hard work and play; our own swimming hole.

Nights of fun, laughter and singing, from somewhere a guitar.

Acres of trees: walnut, persimmon, sycamore, hickory and pawpaw.

Blackberries by the tub full, watermelon, tomatoes, potatoes and corn.

The first fruits and vegetables I could remember.

Now we had enough to eat.

Mom was tired; my brothers helped her in the kitchen.

The doctor came, carrying his black bag.

My brothers told me doctors don't bring babies, and why.

The new baby was a boy; now there were ten brothers.

One girl; I was four years old.

Winter winds whistled through the wooden floors and through the boxing.

At night we snuggled together in beds to keep warm.

Somewhat contented, lots of love, nobody sick.

Spring!

My brothers went swimming on Easter Sunday, always.

Even if they had to break the skifts of ice on the swimming hole.

Daddy went to town to get seeds; horseback, we had no car.

Someday I would get to go to town where big people go.

We made a garden, barefoot; everyone worked and played.

School!

Finally! I get to go to school where my brothers go.

The first special thing that ever happened to me.

New crayons for me, my own tablet and pencil!

Mom made me a new chambray dress.

My big brother carried me the two miles on his back.

Those girls in frilly dresses, blonde curls, blue eyes and pink skin.

I didn't look like other girls look!

With straight bobbed, brown hair, dark eyes, dark, tanned skin; and barefoot.

Girls play different games than boys: jacks, hopscotch, jump rope.

So many things to see: a bicycle, a piano, Jello, the teacher's car.

Books about strange people that were a different color than I was.

Books about lands far away.

They started Church in the schoolhouse on Sunday.

I had never heard of church; the family went in the wagon.

The preacher said we should love thy neighbor as thyself.

Strange; I had never heard of that.

He gave me a little Bible.

I learned to read; the first chapter of Genesis.

Now I knew most everything; I was almost nine.

Spring came.

Mom was tired, in bed; my brother helped with the cooking and homework.

My big brother woke me one morning.

He said we had a new baby sister; he couldn't fool me!

I ran to Mom, who was still in bed.

She showed me; the baby was a girl!

My world was complete; what more could I want.

War! What was that?

Handsome brothers in uniform, going off to protect us, Mom said.

Five of them! But they could die!

Hadn't Grandma died?

She was grouchy, didn't like little kids and smoked a smelly pipe.

I tried to cry when she died, because Daddy was crying, but I couldn't.

How I prayed for my brothers, though I wasn't sure how to pray.

Night after night, year after year, always remembering.

They all came back! Had God really heard?

Daddy worked building defense plants during the war; we moved many times.

Now that the war was over, we could stay in one place.

I could go to one school; I was fourteen.

I was no longer mistaken for one of the boys; that was nice.

It had been fun to be a tomboy or a girl, as I chose.

It was good to be almost a woman.

I had become somebody special in school; good grades, good in sports.

I was outstanding for the first time; it felt good.

Jesus became real to me!

A peace and joy I had never known before!

Daddy. They said he died instantly in the car wreck.

He was so special to me.

He taught me to hope and dream.

I was sixteen.

I didn't want a boyfriend; I had heard my brothers talk about girls!

Bill! He would be a friend; the best friend I could ever have.

I was sixteen! What was happening?

It was good to be a woman.

I was eighteen; we were married.

Bill, my best friend, my lover, the father of my children.

Two sons and two daughters, in that order, in four years.

Time moves so fast!

War again! What kind of war is this?

A son AWOL? It may be said, "The enemy is us."

How brave he was to stand by his convictions!

Another son saved by the lottery.

Both now safe! But what of all the other wasted lives?

"The enemy is us!"

Can it be; our little girls have grown up?

Just yesterday I was braiding their pigtails.

Mom, the tiny matriarch! She has gone to be with her Jesus!

She taught me to have compassion for others.

So much of her is still with me; I shall always miss her.

What? I'm a grandmother?
But grandmothers are old and grouchy and strange; not this one!
I am a woman, a daughter, a mother, a sister, a scholar!
I am a wife, a friend and a lover.
For Bill and me, life is good; most of it is still ahead of us!

Bonnie Lacey Krenning

June 1975

# THE SPUR RANCH DEER

## Caroline Grace

The Spur Ranch deer crowded together in a little grove of trees for warmth. They sensed another snowstorm in the air. The sky had turned gray and overcast, and the deer waited to graze until the sun once again shone brightly.

One mama deer, who was having a baby, laid down in a grassy place shielded from the cold by overhead tree branches. She was a little way from the other deer for privacy but still sheltered from the snowstorm.

The snow was already deep around the grove. Close to it, a Jeep sat stuck in the snow. The boot of the Jeep held many things a ranch hand would need if stranded overnight. There were blankets, a tarp, and rifles for protection from wolves, brown bear, and other predators in the area. In a snowstorm, the predators looked for food. Rifles were necessary for survival.

The driver of the Jeep built an igloo out of snow. It would be much warmer than the interior of the Jeep. The other ranch hands wouldn't miss him until morning. They would then come to look for him. They knew the gray sky showed more snow and would endanger no one else's life by hunting for him until they could see.

Wolves yapped in the distance, so he brought the rifles into the finished igloo with him. He spread the tarp on the wet ground and put the blankets on top. He knew the smell of fresh blood from the mama deer giving birth would attract the wolves and bear around them. So, he pulled some dry grass and added it to an old rabbit warren near Mama Deer. He petted her so that his smell was familiar to her. She would use the warm grass to not only keep the fawn warm but also safely hidden from any danger.

The wolves smelled the human odor, but the night passed with none of them coming close to their little makeshift homes.

Morning came with a new baby fawn snuggled in the dry grass bed. It also brought ranch hands mounted on horses and dragging bales of hay tied to their saddles with a rope. They used the hay and the horses to get the Jeep back on the trail. It worked even though there was more snow on it from the fresh fall of snow during the night.

As he added hay to the fawn's bed and gave Mama Deer some hay to eat, the Jeep driver thought about breakfast and home. The herd could eat the rest of the hay, and life could soon be back to ranching as usual.

## HUMBLE PIE

R. E. Brown

There is a popular exercise in which folks try to establish their intelligence ranking with respect to others. That is perhaps why some TV situation comedies are so popular and enjoy such long runs. All one must do to feel relatively smart or wise is to watch those shows and proclaim, usually to themselves, "that was dumb, I wouldn't have said that, or done that!"

Unfortunately, TV advertising revenue is a function of viewership, the number of regular viewers or addicts. So new, competing shows, are obliged to create situations or characters that are dumber than those of established shows. It is an endless but apparently profitable race to the bottom.

Yet no one wants to contemplate the possibility they may somehow be the dumbest person in the world, or even in the lower quartile.

Consider a scientific rear view.

The number of facts, information, histories, scenarios etc. in the Universe is infinite!

What is Avogrodo's number?

Who was the first to discover Kerosene?

What was the explosive efficiency of the first nuclear bomb?

Is the Kuiper Belt leather or, what?

Where are vortex generators employed?

How far from LA to DC?

Who's on first?

What does the back of my head look like?

And so on...and on...and....

So, let K(universe) represent the infinity of knowledge extant in the Universe.

Let k(me) represent my knowledge and k(you) represent your knowledge.

Further, let k(you) equal 1,000k(me), so that you are a thousand times smarter than I. Since ignorance is simply that which we do not yet know,

my ignorance, $i(me) = \{K(universe) - k(me)\}$,

and yours, $i(y) = \{K(universe) - k(y)\}$,

$= \{K(universe) - 1,000k(me)\}$.

But infinity minus any discrete number, however large, is still infinity

So $i(y) = i(me) =$ infinity!!!!

We are all equally ignorant!!!!

WELCOME TO THE CLUB!!!

# TRIP DOWN THE ALASKA CANADA HIGHWAY
# (the ALCAN)

## July 1958

Joan E. Morrison

Friday, July 1st was my last day of work for six weeks, and our seventh wedding anniversary. The next day was Saturday, July 2nd, my 27th birthday, Erwin and I would head home to Ohio. That was 1958–60 years ago.

July 3rd was special because Alaska was ratified by Congress effective for statehood, and it would become official on January 1, 1959—the 49th State—a historic event. A bonfire was set up in the city park at Anchorage and we passed that on our way out of town.

And July 4th was special too—Independence Day—spent on the road after a night near the Alaska/Canada border.

Erwin got our car all ready for the trip with bug screens on the front, mud flaps on the back, extra tires, extra gas, complete checkup for the car. We planned on being gone for six weeks. I took a vacation from my job and Erwin was going to out of the Air Force at Lockbourne AFB in Columbus where he signed up, finishing a four year tour of duty, and we planned to come back to Anchorage where we would seek civilian employment. I was working at Bendix Radio, a division of Bendix Aviation Corporation based in Maryland, on base at Elmendorf AFB. We were going to pick up Erwin's cousin Charles Humble and his wife Jeanie where he was stationed at an Air Force station near Spokane, Washington.

We would go from Anchorage to Tok Junction at the Alaska-Canada border, 328 miles and 93 to the border, and 1314 to Dawson Creek. From Dawson Creek south to the U.S. border by way of Prince George, B.C. 797 miles. We crossed the border at

Washington state near Spokane. Then we went to Ohio after picking up Charles and Jeanie; plus the Washington to Ohio trip, about 4000 miles.

After leaving Anchorage on the third of July, we spent the first night near Tok Junction, Alaska in a pup tent, with mosquitoes right outside—lots of them. We decided not to use the tent next time. The next night we spent in the car by a lake. It would be another day before we got to Dawson Creek—three days altogether on the Alcan. We had a Milepost, the Guide to the Land of the Midnight Sun, a booklet describing the Alcan Highway.

July 8, 1958, 3:00 pm

Letter home

Dawson Creek British Columbia

While I'm waiting on Erwin to get the car checked, I'll write you about our trip so far. Erwin will ask if they'll take the car now. This morning they said to come back at 3 pm to see if they could take it today. If not, it would have to be tomorrow, and Erwin said we'd have to wait until tomorrow night to leave. He wants to get the carburetor reset for altitudes. The car doesn't have much "pep" or "pickup" on high altitudes or mountains. Thinks that the fuel pump might be at fault. So far, there are no other troubles. The tires are holding up ok. And boy it's a wonder. We've had gravel road since about mile 1300, east of Tok Junction—that's 1300 miles of gravel road. Parts of it was well packed and easy to travel over, and part was loose gravel. Had bumps and chuckholes in parts. All the way it was dusty. Wasn't too bad riding unless we got in back of another car or truck which we would pass.

Dust got in everything not well covered or sealed. Every time we stopped to cook meals we had to wash everything. We've had to change clothes a time or two, too, because the dust makes everything filthy. Probably wouldn't matter about looks as we've only hit about two towns—that's Fort Nelson and Dawson Creek. A person feels bad enough when he's dirty, and with the hot weather makes one feel worse.

We were sure glad to get this motel room last night. My hair was white with dust. We showered, and I washed my hair and changed clothes and washed clothes and dishes. And with that nice soft bed to sleep in I'm feeling human again. I don't have my iron so couldn't wear the clothes I washed out. I bought a pair of toreador pants and sport blouse and CAP, which I hope keeps out some dust, today at one store in Dawson Creek.

Dawson Creek is a nice sized little town—has all the stores one needs. Population 7500—has 8 motels and 5 hotels and 3 movie houses, a radio station and a newspaper. It's the biggest place we've hit since leaving Anchorage. Whitehorse, Yukon Territory, is the only other place to compare with it and it doesn't have a radio station or a newspaper. I think we're on the edge of the frontier now. From here on it should be more civilized. We saw a couple ranches about 50 miles north of here where they raise Herefords. Other than that, there is no use being made of the land that I could see, except maybe logging. There are probably mines—asphalt, and ores of some kind. This place is the end of the line for one railroad. No railroads north of here. After reading my Milepost I guess there are farmlands north of here. There is a wheat mill here anyhow, and there is oil refining, too, I think. At least I know there's one at Ft. St. John 47 miles north of here. We saw its flames shooting up.

We saw several forest fires coming down. Got pictures of them too. It wasn't dangerous, not like you see in the movies. Not dangerous to people that is. There was mostly smoke—just a couple times did I see flame. Once through the binoculars from a distance we could see flames—that fire was pretty big. Then the other time, we had been going by burned out sections where there was still a lot of smoldering smoke coming up out of the ground and I saw a little burst of flames. Some bulldozers had been along and pushed down trees along the road to provide a fire break I suppose so the fire wouldn't spread.

Weather has been sunny and hot. Hit a couple quick rainstorms. We've wished for cloudy weather because we're not used to this hot weather.

There are 790 miles to go before we get to the Washington border. We will pick up Charles and Jeanie if all goes well, at Curlew Air Force Station near Wauconda, Wash. That's just inside the Washington border. After a few hours or maybe a day there, which I expect will be Thursday or Friday, we'll start for Billings, Montana. After a short visit (not more than a day I hope), we'll start for Ohio. I would say about next Sunday we start for Ohio.

Well, I guess that's just about it. Will sign off for now. See you soon. Love to all, Joan

PS. Erwin just got back with the car (6 pm), and he had to get a new fuel pump. They fixed it today, so we'll leave here tonight at midnight for Prince George (255 miles).

On July 8th in Dawson Creek, BC we thought we would have daylight most of the night. I remember little of that night, but we had 250+ miles of road to go to Prince George. It was probably forested with some mountain road, probably paved. Evidently it was okay since I didn't write home about it.

The trip from Dawson Creek south through British Columbia was nice; fresh fruits and vegetables were available. We enjoyed Bing cherries—couldn't get enough. After four years in Alaska without local fresh fruits it was a treat.

**FYI

The Alcan skirts north of the Rocky Mountains. Its access roads to the U.S. southern border of Canada goes west through Prince George, B.C. to Washington and east through Alberta, Canada to Edmonton and Calgary to Great Falls, Montana.

The only town—at that time—on the route was Whitehorse, Yukon Territory, mile 917.4 and is off the highway about a mile and a half. The 1956 milepost said the population was abut 5,000. We stopped off the highway to tour this town.

The milepost stated: "The new two-million-dollar government (Canadian) building was completed in 1954 and several new facilities for visitors have been recently added."

The Yukon River runs by it. There is lots of information about this area in the milepost. Gold rush camps were at the site of Whitehorse.

# THE POET
## Coe Holden

The old man sat motionless with his head in his hands.

Is he asleep or just deep in thought?

Time passes and with no change in expression he starts to jot something down.

Then back to motionless. Silence and time passes.

Then he is wide-eyed and a smile on his face. The words start to appear on the paper as if a strange force was driving the pen.

And when he is through, the old man sits back in his chair, crosses his hands and with a sigh, he says to himself.

"This is finished."

## MEMORIES

Maudyne Cline

I can still remember three little girls who all slept in the same room of our home's large front bedroom, and each girl had a single bed.

Their brother had his own room, and he didn't let them forget it. But the brother was nice about sharing his toys: boys' stuff. By being so nice, they invited him to play with the girls' toys. Examples: iron, ironing board, cash register, cabinets made from orange crates and small unbreakable dishware. The children would set up shop and invite the neighborhood children over to play store. They always seemed to have plenty of empty soup, vegetable and fruit cans to sell.

Their dad would arrive home late, around midnight, as his work schedule varied. After checking on his little angels he retired to the front room and read until mom said it was time to come to bed and rest.

Our son was an alert child and always looking after his younger sister as she loved to investigate everything possible in her new surroundings.

Once she opened all the drawers of his bedroom dresser and tried to climb to the top. Her four-year-old big bother saved her.

Then this same little sister, three and a half years old, thought she would open the car door, jump inside and look around. Her big brother saved the day again and got her out of the car.

Enough for now.

Then several stories later...

The oldest sister who was in high school invited her boyfriend to drive over to our house, so her dad could have a look-see at boyfriend's car problem. Fortunately, right next door to our house was a vacant lot. After several hours of checking the car engine, they discovered a new fan belt was necessary. He had to leave the car sitting in the empty lot for several days.

The boyfriend had just enlisted in the Air Force and was stationed at McConnell Airbase, Wichita, Kansas. He had to wait for three days until his next day off. I don't believe Dad offered his car repair service to the young friends of his darling daughters.

Then the story of the second daughter who just had to self-pierce her earlobes. I believe her best girlfriend was trying to pierce her earlobes at the same time. The girls were racing to see who would win.

So many more stories.

Later…

Sisters jumping off front porch steps, trip to the doctor for stitches. Daughter roller skating and she broke her left wrist.

Brother jumping off backyard shed, playing Superman, and, hooray! Another broken wrist in the family records.

## THE PHOTO ALBUM

Jan Koelsch

"What do I get Mom for Christmas this year?" I asked myself. Getting a gift for her was one of the most difficult things to do each year. She was a woman who could buy anything she could want. She and Dad had always been savers throughout their married lives. Both had worked hard to buy their home, provide whatever my sister and I needed and wanted. They owed no one any money. Part of their legacy was the value of the dollar and the time investment and in giving to other people. For Mom that legacy was the most important thing she could provide.

So, what was her gift going to be this year? The only answer was to make her something she could not exchange. It was a gift that needed customization and personalization. Then the thought came what the gift should be—a photo album.

In the bottom right drawer of her dresser were a multitude of family photos of all shapes and sizes. The photos spanned Mom's lifetime and mine. Rifling through the photos provided humor, some sadness and unexpected moments. There was a history of Christmas and Easter where mother/daughter outfits were the fashion statements of the time. White patent leather shoes and new purses were the accessories of the day. There was that one photo that showed my cousin, Julie about 4 years old, with her right frilly sock and white shoes in the middle of a delicious basket of chocolate candy. The camera caught it all. Then there were photos of the funeral of my grandpa. It took my breath when I saw my grandpa lying in his casket. Those pictures were not ones that were going in that photo album.

The scrapbook chosen for this gift was a white wedding album, about 4 inches thick. There was no way I could ever fill that book, but it was to be a start. Mom could add pictures to it as we celebrated those special times in life. Organizing it would be no small feat. I'm not prone to making snap judgments about too many things. This was something I wanted my mom to treasure as much as I treasured putting it together.

I dedicated the first chapter of the album to my parents; first as single people and then as a couple. Mom had such beautiful, thick long black hair when she was 19. It had a soft natural wave to it. She had such a beautiful smile. It was no wonder Dad fell for her. Then there was that handsome young man with thick, tousled dark hair. That was my dad. He had such a boyish grin that would steal the heart of any young woman. They made a very handsome couple. The picture of a happy young couple walking down the aisle after vows that promised "for better or worse" started the chapter of our family.

The next chapter was me. The baby pictures of a pudgy baby girl with little fat thighs looking like a baby Buddha smiling with all the sweetness of someone whose first name means "God's gracious one." It was a baby born the day after Mom and Grandma had finished Christmas shopping in Wichita. It was a baby that was the second grandchild of Mom's side of the family. This photo was a colorized portrait and had sit on the piano opposite from my sister's baby picture. Both photos sat behind the bronzed baby shoes of our tiny feet. There were pictures of my second birthday with the cake I leaned over, so wanting to put my fingers in the icing. There was a baby doll sitting beside me, but the cake won. The photographer caught it in the black and white pictures. The chapter of me included grade school report cards. There was my first piano recital where I posed for the camera in the community room at the back of the Eureka Federal Bank. Then there were graduation pictures from high school, college and seminary. There were pictures of all the positive events that made me who I was.

Chapter 3 was my sister's chapter, unique to her. There was the tiny newborn baby picture and the photo of the toddler sitting in the child-size rocking chair. She was such a happy little one. Holidays and graduations were celebrated in her chapter, too. It captured her wedding memories as happy times. There were pictures of Kandi, Jason and Val, the only grandchildren my mom and dad would have.

They were the three best gifts a daughter could give to her mother.

Chapter 4 was the grandchildren chapter. What sweet memories those pictures evoked. There was Kandi, the most beautiful baby in the world. She had wrapped all of us around those little fingers and herself around our hearts. There is something special about that first grandchild. Jason with his red hair and love of dressing like a cowboy including his boots was next in line. Jason could get his grandma and his aunt to do most anything for him. Then there was Val. She was the scrawniest baby I had ever seen. Her picture is proof of that statement. She filled out and was the essence of mischief. After all, she had to keep up with her brother and sister. The grandchildren chapter added another dimension to history. It gave depth and richness to the legacy of my sister.

The finished product brought me warmth and tenderness. I hoped Mom would feel the same. There was not much ado about photo albums at the time. It was a collage of family pictures.

Mom was almost speechless when she unwrapped my gift that year. That was a rare accomplishment any time. As she leafed through the pages of memories, it was awesome to see her pause and know she was going back in time to special places with special people. When she finished, she looked at me and simply said thank you. The look in her eyes told me it was a cherished gift—a gift from one heart to another.

## THE GIFT

Donita M Davis

Life was getting a bit harder

For that character, my husband Ray.

Getting out of a chair took effort,

And "I miss driving the car," he'd say.

Daughter Lynette invited the family

To eat lunch with her after church on Sunday.

It was fun. Then we all went home.

But Ray left us around midnight on Monday.

He had no idea he'd be leaving us.

And for sure, neither did I.

At the hospital, I planned to stay with him.

But instead, it was our last good bye.

When they called me in to see him,

I knew he wasn't truly there.

His soul had taken off for heaven,

To the home Jesus said He'd prepare.

I loved that dear man, and I surely miss him.

Thank God, in his youth, he did fervently pray,

"Jesus, I believe in You as my Savior."

Ray is not gone. He's just away.

Up there do believers chat about love?

The birth, death and resurrection of Christ?

Ray will interrupt, "Jesus, thanks for THE GIFT

OF ETERNAL LIFE for which you paid the price."

# CODE 3 REVISITED

## A Continuing Intrigue Story

Lois Ann Seiwert

"Tom! Rosie! Boy, am I glad to see you two! This has been the wildest 48 hours imaginable! I have to keep busy or I start thinking about all the What Ifs and How Comes. Let's go get something to drink and head for the patio. There's some good shade on the east side."

Julie sighed as she settled into her cushioned patio chair. "Iced Cinnamon Mocha Coffee really hits the spot today!" She glanced at her friends. "How is it you are also in Chicago?"

Tom flashed a big grin. "Meetings with our recording engineer for our upcoming release. It went very well. Needless to say, we are excited and anxious." He paused, looking serious. "It is, indeed, a weird coincidence we end up sitting together at the Chicago Art Museum today. I am so glad to see you!"

Julie nodded, sipped her coffee, and reflected on the sequence of recent events. It had started with Eric's ultimatum and the anxious phone call for the Plan Code 3, needed immediately. Then moving her things from his house, a midnight flight to an unknown hideaway, and becoming an alias persona riding the midnight train to Chicago. Her circumstances had changed dangerously in a short time. Fortunately, Tom and Rosie had prepared for such a situation.

She had handled her sudden escape. Now she had to consider creating some new arrangements in her life. Eric was out of her life, permanently. And maybe that was okay. It wasn't the first time this had happened, and life had always opened new doors for her.

Rosie piped up, "I'm ready to go see that new Impressionistic Art Collection that just opened. How about you?"

"Sounds great!" chorused Tom and Julie as they rose from their chairs.

******

After touring the exhibit, they returned to the outside patio. Julie smiled as she sat down. "That was pretty neat. Some of the paintings are beautiful—so peaceful. It's like you're sitting on a hillside viewing the scene through a haze of summer humidity." She wrinkled her nose. "Some of them, though, are just a bunch of lines and daubs of color. I couldn't tell what was in the picture. Those I could do without."

Tom interrupted Julie. "I was thinking about all of us getting back to Seattle. Our plan is to drive the van to Brian's place in Idaho. It's deep in the backwoods about an hour's hike from the hideout we own. He has his own airstrip and recording studio and also does sculpting with local stone. He has a car stored for us that we want to get back to Seattle. I planned to spend a couple of days visiting after we get the car ready to travel."

Tom continued, "If you want to come along with us, you and Rosie can travel together to Seattle. We have enough space in the den—with the rest of your stuff—which you can use until you get settled elsewhere."

Rosie piped in, "Sounds great! We just need to figure out where to meet you in the morning, early! There is that park a couple of blocks from the train station. Maybe that would work."

Julie moved her chair closer to the table. "That beats riding the train alone. And I'll get to see some of the country as we go west. I have seen little of Idaho or eastern Washington."

She thought for a moment. "I know someone in Spokane that we could possibly stay with overnight. It's one of our classmates—Marty. She has two kids and a nice comfy house on the edge of the city."

As her friends looked agreeable, she said, "Sounds like a good plan! I need to call my mom, but I will wait until I find out if there is space available at Harry's Hostel House in Seattle where I have roomed before. And I want to call into the office. I have four days of vacation left, but I think I will check in when we get back."

"Harry's Hostel House?" Rosie asked.

Julie smiled in memory. "The thing that's so nice about Harry's—you get two large rooms with big windows and a bath. And it is within walking distance of the office, a post office, a corner grocery store, and a bus stop.

"So, what time do you want to meet in the morning? I think the merry-go-round there in the park would be a good place. There's a picnic table nearby."

"Seven should work great," answered Rosie. "And we have enough food to get us down the road for most of tomorrow."

Julie shifted in her chair, staring off into space. "Do you remember that one picture of the two girls sitting under a tree reading a book together? It brought back memories of school days in Coon Creek, Illinois."

She grinned and laughed. "Remember how we always added 'about an hour south of Chicago in the middle of the corn fields'? Our little library had an arrangement with the Chicago system. Every Friday they would bring down a van load of books on loan. We would check them out for two weeks—six max per person. We would ride bikes or roller skate over on Friday afternoon to check out some new books. Then we'd go to the park, sit under the big shade tree and read half of them before we even got home."

Tom looked up from the book on Renaissance musical instruments he'd bought in the museum's gift shop. "I didn't know that you two grew up together—in Cook Creek, Illinois, no less. I knew the story about your finding each other while standing side by side ordering hot dogs at the Vancouver Music Festival. That was quite a surprise!"

Julie continued the story. "We had both ordered the same hot dog, except I wanted onions and she didn't. I looked up to see this person beside me and recognized her profile. I knew that I knew it, but just couldn't place her."

She smiled at Rosie, who was nodding at the memory. "She looked at me and got a strange look on her face. In less than two seconds we both were crying, laughing, screaming and hugging all at the same time! It had been 12 years since we had lost contact. After college graduation, I had left for Japan on a language scholarship to teach English and Rosie had gone to Africa with the Peace Corps."

"Yea, we lived only two blocks apart and met at a preschool class when we were four years old," Rosie joined in. "We were best friends throughout school. We did our homework together and had sleepovers on the weekends. We even talked our moms into having lunch together during the summers—one day at her house, the next day at mine."

Julie continued the explanation. "There was water ballet practice in the morning, choir practice on Sunday morning an hour before services, and cheerleading lessons at the school gym three days a week. The tryouts were in late August, right before school started and everybody wanted to be a cheerleader."

She glanced at Rosie. "Remember the year we went to state competitions and came home with a second-place ribbon for the small school classification? That was really neat! We had our picture in the Chicago Tribune Sports section and were the talk of the town for a while. In high school we both got summer jobs at the Jackson's diner downtown on Main Street and did some volunteering at the library and swimming pool."

Sadness filled her voice. "It all ended when Rosie's dad got a job promotion. They had to move to New Jersey—just two weeks before our senior year. We were so broken hearted. I know I cried for days. Her father wouldn't hear of her staying at my house, so she could finish high school with our classmates."

Julie paused, swallowing down the painful memory. "We wrote each other every week that year and kept in contact all throughout college.

She majored in English and planned to teach and get a master's degree. I completed a double major in Accounting and International Language Studies. We planned on getting jobs in the same city."

Rosie started to smile as Julie continued, "It was so great growing up in a small town. You could go anywhere, and you knew most of the people if you had a problem. I hear that has changed now. A lot more people live there now and drive into the Chicago area for their jobs. Some of them are not particularly friendly."

Julie paused, shifted in her chair and changed the subject. "I have a How Come question. How is it that you saw a need to outline escape plans from Eric's house, anyway?"

"It's a long story," Tom answered, his brow furrowing. "We became involved with a Legitimate Underground Cadre when we were working on getting a music profile. It provided extra income for us. Then some guy from Florida named Rodney talked his way into the group."

"I never liked him from the beginning," Rosie inserted, sounding frustrated.

"He turned out to be not trustworthy, stealing clients and lying about his activities and whereabouts," Tom explained. "The music was generating income now, and we were working on our first recording. I decided it was time to move out of the realm—much to Rosie's relief."

He shared a look with Rosie. "We kept in contact with a couple of friends about what was happening and where. When we heard Eric's connected with the LA scene, we became alarmed. Some checking confirmed our worst fears. This was big time activity with laser guns that disable phones, electricity and security systems and deactivate deadbolts and door locks for entry. And self-combusting body bags that disappear, leaving no trace of evidence."

Looking at Julie, he said, "We were sure that you knew none of this and we didn't want to alarm you at that point. But I sure am glad that we got a plan set up with you and that you're sitting here talking with us!"

Julie had trouble hearing all of this about someone she'd had so much fun with. She blinked back tears, feeling foolish. "I hope you know how much I appreciate your efforts for my safety." She heaved a sigh. "I'm ready to go back to my room and get packed up for tomorrow's journey. Get some sleep. You said seven as I remember. That will work for me."

"Done deal!" exclaimed Rosie, looking glad to have the difficult conversation over with. "See you in the morning at the merry-go-round. And here's a sandwich and a bag of chips that I had put in my bag when we left the room this afternoon."

Julie rose from her chair, eager to be alone for a while. "Thanks! Your kindness and help are really special to me!"

******

Tom looked up from his egg and cheese biscuit. "Good morning, Julie!" Then he frowned a bit. "You look a little ragged. Did you not sleep well last night?"

She shook her head, knowing she looked bad. A glance in the mirror had told her that. "I didn't sleep well at all. Too many things going around in my head. I realized that I had been so involved with the music projects and overtime at work that I had missed the clues that things were changing between Eric and myself."

She paused for a moment. "Recently, he had told me that he was losing interest in the music projects. He didn't want to go to any more music festivals. And he was planning to go to LA for a rally the weekend that I was going to the Winfield Walnut Valley Music Festival for the songwriting contest."

She blew out a breath, explaining, "We had some tense words. I finally told him that I wasn't trying to tell him what he was supposed to be doing with his life. I would finish the songs myself and take his name off the application."

Julie could see now that there had been other things happening that showed Eric's interests had changed. He'd gone out with the guys more often in the evenings, till late. He seemed restless and easily upset. A bad flu hit him after he lost his job in a merger deal. After that he had started wiping down everything in the house with antibacterial spray. But she'd just let it all pass as a phase he was going through. She'd asked him once if he was feeling okay, but he hadn't given her a clear answer.

She shook off the troubled thoughts, the regrets. "It's easy to be angry with myself, but it's over with now. I can't change what happened, so I must move on and figure out what happens next."

When Tom looked up, she forced a smile. "Are we ready to hit the road? I'm sure we want to get ahead of the traffic. And I'm ready to head west for the open country and some mountains!"

As the three friends walked toward the van, Rosie glanced back at the picnic table. "I don't see that we left anything behind. We gassed up last night ant washed the windows so they would be clear. So we should be good to go!"

Tom opened the rental van doors for Julie, showing her the sleeping bag, sheet, and foam pad they had picked up at the thrift store for the trip home. He looked concerned. "I need to get up front and look at my maps one more time," he said as Julie put her bags on the floor.

As she climbed in, happy to be off her feet, Rosie pointed out the bright red Coke cooler. "There are some bananas and boxes of rice milk in that cooler. And I have bags of granola and some bowls and silverware in the Chicago Cubs tote bag so you can fix yourself something to eat. Then, hopefully, you can get some rest. I will have some breakfast later when we get out on the highway. I need to keep check on the maps for Tom."

Rosie had a big, happy grin on her face. "Look out Interstate 90, here we come!" she exclaimed as she closed the van doors and headed up to join Tom. She turned to check on Julie one more time, reminding her to lock the van doors, as Tom pulled out into the traffic.

# I HAVE FALLEN, AND I CAN'T GET UP

## Beverly J. Hamilton

A year after being widowed I came to the real understanding of what it means to live alone.

Earlier in my life I had both knees replaced with artificial implants. They instructed me to never get on my knees even to pray! This had not been a problem until I fell out of my bed.

Yes, that's right, I'm seventy-seven years old, and I fell out of my bed at 2:30 AM. I awoke with a thud!

Dazed, I lie there trying to figure out what had just happened and where I was. Slowly, I realized; I fell out of bed!

For several months now I had announced to my close girlfriends that I planned to join one of those online dating services. I was lonely and hoped to meet some nice older gentleman who was also lonely.

As I lay there on the floor, I wished for a strong man to help me up out of this situation! I realized I would need assistance to become vertical again. I tell myself to stay calm you can think of a solution but after feeble attempts at getting up I decided I would have to call for help, but who?

I scoot to the desk and retrieve my cell phone that's charging there. Remembering its 3:00 AM by now still too early to wake anyone, the only other option is to call 911. I dial, and a kind voice comes on the line, "What's your emergency?"

I explain my situation and the kind voice asks repeatedly "Are you hurt?"

I assure her that I am ok and only my pride hurts! She asks for my address and information how the EMS people can enter my home to assist me. I describe to her where a key is hidden.

Five minutes later I hear the vehicle pull into the driveway.

Still lying on the floor, I straighten my hair and smooth my flannel night gown thinking if I had only known I would fall out of bed I would have fixed my hair and worn my lacy nighty!

Entering the house, the two firemen holler asking for directions.

I reply, "In here on the floor." Looking up from the floor the firemen appear to be seven feet tall and all muscle! Visions of Paul Bunion come to mind! They have so many items of interest hanging from their belts it would seem troublesome to even walk.

The older one asks if I am injured or hurting anywhere. I assure him, only my pride is bruised. I apologize for my situation and explain how grateful I am for their assistance. They assure me they do this kind of rescue often and it is just part of their job. They asked if I could stand on my own if they lifted me up? I assured them I believed I could. They then each grabbed an arm and on three I was up and back among the vertical once more.

At this point I became emotional and asked if I could give them a hug.

They smiled. If you find yourself in an unfortunate situation such as this, the take away from this experience is stay calm and don't hesitate to call 911. They are kind and helpful and its part of their job.

## BOOK CLUB LADIES

### Gwendolyn Eldridge Gandy

It's a warm morning and already sunny. The third Thursday which means our book club will meet at 5:30pm at Brenda's house. This month is her turn to host our book club. She has offered to serve a light dinner for us. By us, I mean the other six ladies in our club and myself. P.K., Taffy, Lois, Fran, Kay and Brenda were all club members. I (Lynn) met the other ladies through Brenda. We all have a love and joy for reading, so they asked me to join the book club.

We are a lively and fun group. All of us are retired and interesting people, who plan to make this time of our lives a great and awesome adventure. We like to read good books along with a glass of tasty wine. In fact, the name of our book club is "Reading Between the Wines." True, seniors do have all the fun and we are great examples of that, and proud of it.

I had stopped by Brenda's house earlier today to give her a helping hand getting things ready for the meeting this evening. Her eyesight isn't what it used to be. Nobody over eighty has the sight they did at twenty. Often, she gets things a little confused. Brenda informed me she had copied a recipe off of the computer. I worried about her ability to see and copy from the computer. As she said, who could mess up a chicken casserole.

Brenda had put all the ingredients into her new clay pot casserole dish. It was ready for the oven. The casserole dish looked great, but the smell was a little fishy. Oh well. If you put an appealing dish on the table, if your eyes and mind tell you it looks good, then your taste buds will assume it will also taste good. That is what they say on all the TV cooking shows. After a few glasses of wine who will remember how it tastes!

Lois stopped by to drop off the dinner rolls and to look at Muffy, Brenda's cat who wasn't feeling well. Lois also mentioned that the casserole sitting in the oven smelled a little fishy. Brenda said it couldn't because it is a chicken casserole.

Lois and I looked at each other and smiled. I thought to myself, I will need to eat before I come back this evening. I am sure Lois was thinking the same thing.

Muffy had moved little during the day and Brenda told Lois that she was very worried about him. Lois told her to call Dr. Johnson her vet. After talking with him, he told Brenda he would stop by to look Muffy over on his way home. He only lives a door down from Brenda's house.

Lois and I left to go home, so we could get ready for the book club and dinner later. As we walked home, we talked about the fishy smell and sick Muffy. We both decided to only eat salad and bread but have lots of wine.

At 5:30pm everyone had arrived at Brenda's. The food was on the table and we were all ready to have a great time. In the kitchen Muffy was still on the floor when Gail stumbled over him. He didn't move or make a sound. Even her screams caused no reaction from him. Muffy just laid there on the floor. Brenda picked him up and hugged him, still no movement. She started to cry, then we all cried.

Luckily someone heard the doorbell ringing through the crying. It was the doctor. Brenda rushed him into the kitchen. While he worked on the cat, we all continued to cry and pray.

Later what seemed like an eternity, we heard a low moaning noise, and everybody stopped crying to listen.

"He's alive! He lives!" Lois shouted.

Gail said "Hallelujah!"

Brenda cried and kept saying, "It is a miracle! It's a miracle! He's not dead!"

Dr. Johnson came into the living room to quiet us all down. He asked Brenda if he could look into her refrigerator. He found a new white box with Muffy's special milk. Sitting next to the milk was another white box with "White Chocolate Wine" written on it. Brenda had gotten the boxes mixed up. Muffy hadn't died, he was just drunk.

We were all happy to have Muffy back. Dr. Johnson said he wouldn't be feeling really good until sometime tomorrow. He promised Brenda that he would stop by and check on Muffy in the morning.

When Brenda had regained herself and served dinner, she fixed a plate for Muffy. He hadn't eaten all day and was starving. He gulped up the casserole off his plate. It still smelled fishy.

We could only hope whatever mystery meat she was serving tasted good. We now knew for sure it wasn't chicken. What other mistakes had Brenda made today? We could only guess.

Louis and I stuck to our plan of salad, bread, and wine...and more wine. We all were a little tipsy by the time our book club discussion started.

I shared a quote with the ladies I ran across today. It said our club was like a bra because we give so much support to each other. How true.

## AT WORKDAY'S END

### Bonnie Creekmore

Thank you, Lord,
For rest so sweet
When I've been standing
On my feet
Cleaning halls
And mopping rooms,
Hauling carts
And pushing brooms.
The beeper calls—
No break for me.
Bedpans needed
On Six and Three.
Linens stacked
And heavy too,
Open the chute—
I'll stuff it through.
Trash is waiting,
On each floor—
I get one
Then there's two more.

But, wait a minute.
When I clock out
In my mind
There is no doubt
There will be a check
In Thursday's mail,
Come wind or rain
Or sleet or hail.
And I've made friends,
Helped someone,
Even joked
And had some fun.
Talked with doctors,
Nurses, too.
They're glad I'm here
To help them through.
I'll clock out
When day is done,
Go home and think
Of tomorrow's run.
It isn't long
Till I'm fast asleep,
Resting these
Poor aching feet.

## THE OTHER HALF OF ME
### Beverly J. Hamilton

Years have passed and here we are—two souls lost
Looking for a star—two drifting alone from afar
Then one day, there you are—with smiles, soft words
And gentle touch—All the things that mean so much.
Something sparks within us and we know what will be
We both have feelings, "I love you and you love me."
Oh darling, you can see, you are the other half of me!
When we are close, you can see, all that is we can be.
Our love has made us whole—no longer drifting souls.
Now, my dear, we can see, you're the other half of me.
Time and your passing have taken its toll—your smile, your heart,
Your soul—are gone. But memories will linger on.
For you were the other half of me.
Oh darling, yes you were the other half of me.
When we were close, we could see all that would be.
Our love made us whole—no longer drifting souls
It's plain to see, you were the other half of me.
Oh yes, darling, you were the better half of me.

## I WENT OUT TO LOOK AT THE SKY
### Martha Williams Prentice

I went out to look at the sky

as I often do

it was black and deep

with no moon

the stars piercing white

Venus hung close and low in the west

... and I thought of you.


The air made its presence known

in fine misty dew

cold, without movement

against my skin

quickening my awareness

of the beauty of stillness

... and I wanted you.

# IF WE SEE YOU

## Sharon Lee Brown

There are three of us emergency nurse friends who like to share expenses at seminars. Charly is a Triage Nurse whose hobby is target shooting, at home she has a permit to carry. Janis is super smart, took karate for two years. She has an "I can handle anything" attitude. I'm Sue, a good old hands on efficient nurse.

We arrived in our second-floor room close to dark. Across the street was a park where we were watching homeless humans burrowing in for the night. A terribly sad sight.

Suddenly we were witnessing a man bludgeoning another man to death. Hard to believe our eyes. We were aghast when he turned and looked up at us.

We jumped back and turned off the light. And we hurried down to the lobby to report the crime.

The police arrived and found the dead man. We tried to give a description but were not much help. "A big man with a hat." What we knew was that he saw us.

We asked the desk to move us to another room but there were no vacancies. The police told us to keep our curtains closed and go about our business. He was probably far away by now.

There would be little sleep without a plan. We barred the door with a chair. Thankfully there wasn't an adjacent room door. The three lamps were heavy and we could use them for defense. Nurses are used to shifts, so we took our turns while the others slept.

The night was quiet, and we were up early to go to our classes. The plan had been to walk the mile to the conference, but we took a cab. After dinner, we took another cab ride back.

We insisted someone check the room before we went inside. The scrawny, nervous desk guy said it was clear. Same routine: barred door, lamps handy, shifts to allow for sleep.

Three quiet nights. The fourth day we were relaxed with only two more nights, then home.

Charly was on watch and yelled to wake us up as a large man was forcing the door open. He tripped on the chair.

Janis jumped out of bed, grabbed the lamp and let him have it on his back.

Charly's lamp got him on the arm.

Mine whacked him on his head.

He was out. The noise alerted someone who called the police.

People and police were praising us and impressed with our actions as they took the man away in an ambulance.

Janis appeared calm; Charly glowed with pride. Not me. I couldn't stop shaking and crying.

We knew if we saw him, he saw us.

## TALKIN' PROPER

Bonnie Lacey Krenning

I started to the one-room country school a year earlier than normal, at five years old. The new experience scared and excited me. Some students were as big as men and women. Having moved into the area less than a year before, some kids didn't know that there was a girl in the family of ten boys with four in school. It seemed everyone looked out for me.

My brothers had taught me before, at home, to write and say my numbers to one hundred and to write and say my ABCs; and the teacher soon realized that. A year younger than the other girl in my class, I was ahead of her in what I knew, even though her mother was a teacher in another school.

I soon noticed that the teacher talked so pretty and used words that I had never heard before. She said isn't instead of ain't, potatoes instead of 'taters, and tomatoes instead of 'maters. There were also many other new words. I soon tried to talk like the teacher.

This seemed to annoy my brother two years older than I and he sometimes acted like he had the right to manage me. He would say, "Quit tryin' to be so proper!" At home, when he heard me trying to talk like my teacher, he would grab me by my forearm and pull me, resisting, to where Mom worked. He would say, "Mom! Bonnie's talkin' proper agin!" Mom would usually say, "Now, Bonnie, quit tryin' to be so fancy."

By summer, after my first year in school, I had learned many of the new words by learning to read and listening to my teacher. I sometimes, yes often, used them to annoy my brother. Sometimes he seemed to realize and accept that I would continue doing it.

One day that summer, when I was six years old, I had finished drying the breakfast dishes for Mom and she said I could go outside and play. My brother was hoeing in the garden on the ridge above the house; I went up to there.

I asked him, "What are you hoeing?"

"Sweet 'taters," he answered.

I told him, "You're supposed to say sweet potatoes."

He yelled at me, "Git back to the house!" When I didn't leave he picked up a clod of dirt and threw at the ground by me, not meaning to hit me, but throwing dust on my bare feet. That made me mad! I leaned forward, clinched my fists and said, "You son of a bitch!"

He glanced at me and threw the hoe down, grabbed me by my upper arm with one hand and my wrist with the other and pulled me toward the house. He yelled at me, "Yur gonna git a whoopin'!"

He scared me and I said, "Why are you so mad? Was I talking proper again?"

"I'm tellin' Mom! Yur gonna git a whoopin'!" he said walking fast.

When we got inside the kitchen where Mom was working, my brother told her what I said. She looked startled and surprised, looking straight at me. "Where did you hear those words?" I told her the neighbor boys sometimes said them on the way home from school when they were mad and fighting each other.

She said, "Those are not nice words! Don't ever say them again." She didn't say whether the words were proper, but I never said them again. She told my brother to stop holding my arm and when I told her that he had thrown a dirt clod at me she scolded him.

My brothers were forbidden to use bad language around me, so he seemed disappointed that Mom wasn't mad at me and I didn't "get a whoopin'" like he would have if he had said the same words.

# THE HAY HOOK KILLER OF WHITE OAK MOUNTAIN

Gerald McCoy

I was visiting family and friends in Waldron, Arkansas. It was late fall, and the leaves that stubbornly clung to their trees displayed breathtaking beauty. Indian summer afternoons were giving way to cool fall nights, which segued into frosty Ozark mornings.

I was at an aunt and uncle's home on a Friday night. They live between Waldron and Booneville about a mile off the blacktop at the foot of White Oak Mountain. We played Rook when we all got together, and some of our card games were legendary. On this particular Friday night, we were working on a good one when the phone rang.

The Little River County Sheriff called and said there had been a murder on the back side of White Oak. Since Sheriff Parker grew up with my dad, he knew I had a law practice in Wichita. The County Attorney of Little River County had never handled a homicide, so Sheriff Parker thought maybe I could help him a little. Even though most of my background was in civil law, I did have some experience in criminal investigations.

I said, "Sure." My dad, my uncle and I headed for the door.

To get to the crime scene, it was about a 45-minute drive in my uncle's Jeep. The journey was filled with switchbacks and forks in the road. Eventually, dirt roads turned into logging trails. The headlights pierced the night and made the overhead tree limbs look like an endless black tunnel. The surrounding woods were pitch dark.

We stopped next to a small shack about 50 yards off the road. A sad looking three-legged dog barked at us as we approached the front porch. "Shut up, Tripod!" Sheriff Parker yelled, and the dog hobbled out of the way.

When we got to the door, I stepped into the shack, and I stepped back in time.

I was stunned by the poverty—hard, grinding poverty. The shack was a small square structure with two door openings on the far wall. One door opened to a room that was used as a kitchen, and the other door opened to a room that was used as a bedroom. In the kitchen was an old barrel that was filled with wood and was covered by a metal grate. The barrel served as a cook stove, as well as a source of heat and light. A water bucket sat on a small table by a window. One of the window panes had been broken, and a piece of cardboard had been wedged into the frame in its place. A rickety old table with two wooden chairs was the only other furniture in the room.

The bedroom was in even worse shape. There was an old bed that had a soiled, filthy mattress and no bedding. No other furniture was in the room. Old boxes in the corner held rags that were used as clothes.

There was a sofa in the living room, but no one sat on it. The cushions were torn, and springs were exposed. There was a chair in the corner that was occupied by a giant man-child. He said nothing and looked at no one. He just rocked back and forth on the chair and clutched what was probably the only toy he'd ever had. It was a small wind-up toy farmer. You could wind it up, set it down, and the toy farmer would walk across the floor.

The cabin walls were lathed, but the plaster had long since fallen off. One naked light bulb suspended from exposed wires and hung from the living room ceiling. The way to turn the light on and off was to twist the bulb in the socket, but you had to be careful not to touch exposed wires while you did it.

Lying in the middle of the living room floor was a beautiful girl with the face of an angel. She had long blonde hair and clear blue eyes that were frozen open in a lifeless stare. Embedded in her back was a hay hook that had been savagely twisted. She is forever five years old.

Her mother was a skinny, middle-aged woman with stringy gray hair. A few teeth were missing; those that remained ones were yellow and crooked. She was crying hysterically and refused to be consoled. "He kilt my baby!" she was screaming. "He kilt my baby girl!" She said it over and over again.

It seemed like it was 30 minutes before she calmed down enough to talk to us. "What did you see?" Parker asked.

"A man was here today," she said.

"Who was he?" Parker asked.

"I don't know," she sobbed. "I ain't never seed him a fore, but he sure liked little Pearl." She started screaming again. "Now he's kilt my baby! He's kilt little Pearl!"

"Take it easy. Take it easy." Parker tried to sound as soothing as he could. "Just tell me what happened."

The woman caught her breath. "A man came by today. He said he was hot, so I give him some water." She went on, "He said he worked oil wells in Louisiana, and he was goin' to Oklahoma to find work. He said can he take Pearl with him, and I said, 'No, she's too little.'"

"Did he seem angry?" Parker asked.

"No," she said.

"What did he look like?" Parker asked.

"He was a little bald headed fella with buck teeth."

"What was he wearing?"

"Overalls and a straw hat."

"Anything else?" Parker asked.

"Well, he talked funny," she said.

"How did he talk funny?" Parker asked.

"I don't know." She shrugged her shoulders. "He just talked funny."

"He's Cajun," I said. Everyone looked at me, and I felt a little uneasy.

I had been listening to the interrogation, but I had my back to them and was looking out the front door. The young County Attorney was a kid who had never been to a crime scene, and this one was particularly grisly. He was out in the yard visibly shaking. Tripod was barking and raising cane. I was listening as Parker resumed his questioning.

"Then what happened?"

"Just a fore suppertime I went to git some wood," she said. "It was about dark when I got back, and there was Pearl," she continued. "He kilt her," she sobbed.

"Did you see anything?" Parker asked.

"No."

"Did you hear anything?" Parker said.

"No."

"Did he see anything?" Parker pointed at Man-Child, who was still rocking on the chair holding his toy farmer.

"Oh, no," she said, "He can't talk about it."

"Is there anything else?" Parker asked.

"No," she said.

We were walking out as the ambulance crew and the coroner were arriving. No one said a word until we got to our vehicles. "What do you think?" Parker asked.

"Your County Attorney can't handle the case," I said matter-of-factly. "If you don't get evidence or a confession, you're dead in the water."

"I know," said Parker. "I'll bring some people up here tomorrow and see if we can find something."

I said, "I'll check bus schedules into Oklahoma." They said not much else the rest of the evening.

******

Parker and two deputies were back on White Oak at sunrise. I stayed in Waldron and helped the County Attorney. We prepared information sheets for Arkansas and Oklahoma State Troopers.

By now, crime reports had hit the radio. "Pearl Ann Turner, aged five years, was murdered in her home in rural Little River County, Arkansas last night," the reporters would say. "The police are seeking a 'Person of Interest.' He is a slightly built man, 5'7" to 5'9" tall. His weight is approximately 145 pounds. He was last seen wearing blue denim overalls and a straw hat. Identifying characteristics include buck teeth and a Cajun accent. He is thought to be seeking employment in Oklahoma oil fields. If you see a person fitting this description, do not approach the individual yourself, but immediately contact your local law enforcement or call Arkansas Crime Stoppers." Everyone was looking for "The Hay Hook Killer of White Oak Mountain."

Someone thought they saw him hitchhiking on Highway 71 outside of Fort Smith. The Arkansas Highway Patrol found nothing. Someone else thought he boarded a bus to Spiro. The Oklahoma State Police went to the Greyhound station, but no one matching that description was on the bus. It was as though this drifter had vanished into thin air.

I went to Sheriff Parker's office on my last afternoon in town. "Are you leaving tomorrow?" he asked me.

"Yeah," I said. "I've got a court appearance on Thursday, and I need to be ready for it."

"I'll be glad when we find this guy," he said.

"Oh, he'll surface eventually." I was sure of it. "When he does, I hope you've got enough to get a conviction."

"Me, too," he said as he sighed.

"I'd like to go back to White Oak one more time," I said. "I just want to make sure I haven't missed anything."

"Well, I can't go out there today," he said. "Can you get there and back without me?"

"I think so," I said.

"Don't be up there after dark," he cautioned. "You don't know the roads all that well, and those people don't know you at all." He continued, "Remember, there are more guns than phones on that mountain."

I told him I'd be careful and headed out the door.

******

It was mid-afternoon when I found my way back to the shack. Tripod barked dutifully when I got out of my pickup. "Hello, Tripod," I said as I walked to the house.

Man-Child met me at the door. He was at least 6'5" and all muscle. I wondered what he'd been eating, but then I decided I didn't want to know. The mind of a child was housed in the body of a giant.

"Momma, that nice boy from Kansas is here," he called out.

A voice from around the corner said, "Well, bring him in."

"I'm heading back home tomorrow," I said. "I was wondering if I could take one last look around."

"Sure," she said. "Just help yourself."

I went outside and began looking around. I was looking for anything that would tie this particular killer to this particular crime. I was hoping to find a tobacco tin, a scrap of paper, a button from overalls, anything that would help. I was quickly losing daylight, and remembering Sheriff Parker's warning, I decided to abandon my search.

I knocked on the door. Pearl's mother said, "Come on in." I stepped inside. "Did you find anything?" she asked hopefully.

"No," I said. "But thanks for letting me look around."

"That's okay," she said. "I'm makin' supper." A fire was going in the barrel, and something raw was on the table. "You want me to fix you a plate?"

"No, thanks," I said without hesitating. "I've got to take off."

I was watching Man-Child play with his toy farmer. He'd wind the doll's crank, set him on the floor, and then jump and cheer as the doll took his mechanical steps.

About the third time I watched this, the toy farmer walked across the faded blood stained chalk outline in the middle of the floor. He stepped into a crack in the floor and fell. Man-child immediately stopped jumping and laughing.

"Oh, no," he said slowly. He walked over, stooped down, and picked up the toy. As he stood up, he gently brushed the light bulb which caused it to slowly swing back and forth. The swinging light took his face in and out of the shadows. It seemed he changed as the light changed. Gone was the child-like innocence. Replacing it was a demon made all the more sinister by the swinging shadow. As I watched him slowly twist the key in the doll's back, I remembered the twisted hay hook in Pearl's back. Man-Child looked up at me and snarled, "I gots to be careful with this one," he said. "I broke uh other one."

That's when I realized the truth about "The Hay Hook Killer of White Oak Mountain." In an instant, I understood everything. The night of the murder, Pearl's mother said Man-Child couldn't talk about it. That wasn't his grief; it was her orders. Then there was Tripod. He barked at everybody, but he didn't bark the day of the murder. The mother said she didn't hear a thing, and now I understood why. The dog didn't bark because the drifter never came. The Cajun didn't vanish; he was never there in the first place.

Without taking my eyes off Man-Child, I started to back up. I swallowed hard, but I was still numb with terror!

The mother came around the corner. She was looking down into a bowl of something that she was stirring. As she slowly raised her eyes to meet mine, I saw a single tear rolling down her cheek. "Please don't take my boy, mister," she pleaded. "He's all I got left."

I was so gripped by fear that I couldn't speak. I merely nodded. I whirled around and ran out of the shack. I tripped over Tripod; he yelped, and I fell. I scrambled to my feet and staggered to my truck. Tripod was barking, and Man-Child was watching. I cranked the engine until it finally fired.

It was full dark when I left, and I still don't know how I got off that mountain. But when I hit blacktop, I laid rubber for a hundred feet. I got back to Waldron and went straight to my motel room. I started taking stuff out to my truck; I didn't even bother to pack. I just threw things in the cab.

I went to the desk and said, "I'm checking out."

"Right now?" asked the clerk.

"Right now," I answered. "I've got to get home."

"It's after check out time," she stammered. "I'll have to charge you for the night."

"That's fine." I was in no mood to talk.

As I was signing my credit card voucher, the clerk said, "That's too bad about that little girl on White Oak."

"Yeah, it's a tragedy," I said without looking up.

"Do you think they'll ever catch him?" she asked.

I looked up. She really was a sweet old lady, and I felt bad about being so abrupt with her. I shook my head a little and said, "I doubt it."

"Oh, that's too bad," she said. "Well, you have a safe trip back to

Wichita." I thanked her and left.

As I drove away, I thought about what I'd say to Sheriff Parker the next time we would speak on the phone. Would I tell the truth or make up a lie? I was thinking about this as I was driving down the highway. I saw White Oak Mountain silhouetted against the night sky. It looked so peaceful and serene like this. But that serenity couldn't make me forget the terror I felt just one hour earlier.

Now, if you're sightseeing in Arkansas, there's a lot of nice scenery. White Oak Mountain is beautiful; if you want to take it in that's fine. Just get off the mountain before the sun goes down.

# THE NEXT JOURNEY, RETIREMENT!
## Money Can't Buy Time
### Rochelle Boster

Embrace retirement, cherish the wisdom gleaned from the past.

Move forward with certainty you have accomplished a job well done!

Honor the legitimate loss you feel for the routine

you wove into each day for many years.

It is okay to be sad or fearful, but leave those feelings

behind as just temporary moments.

Rather than remorse, celebrate your successes.

Including the many people, each with their own stories,

that have been the foundation for this life's journey.

The lives you touched and cared about, should be badges of pride,

fulfillment, and satisfaction for you.

You not only touched lives, but you made a difference,

physically, mentally, and yes spiritually.

With your encouragement you gave them tools,

and more importantly, hope to find a new normal.

**Starla Criser**

The time has come to revel in the latest new beginning,
anticipate the possibilities, not as have to's, but as maybe's!
Leave no day without at least one "aha" thought, action, or deed!
Spend time in lavish abandonment, and money with frugality!
As you feel your way through changes you are about to
experience, grasp things that feel right.
Tickle your creative brain with ideas so fresh and new
your skin is goose bumpy electric.

Embrace this next journey! Make it your next success!

*for Susan and all other lucky retirees*

## LISTEN, I HEARD A BIRD THIS HOUR
### Martha Williams Prentice

Listen, I heard a bird this hour;
look, there grows a rosy flower.

    A cloud glides 'cross the pearl blue sky,
    a lioness with head held high.

        Was that a gentle breeze I felt
        that brought me fragrant gift to smell

            and stir my soul to sing and dance
            with beauty, wonder and inward glance?

# WINNER

Starla Criser

What does one say about a T-shirt that only wanted to please its owner? It longed to be the first choice taken from the large collection of T-shirts. It dreamed of being taken from the closet over and over and over. It feared being forgotten, ignored, one day not being suitable for wearing any longer.

What do you say about a T-shirt that spent its life proudly proclaiming "Winner" across its front?

You say it was a good shirt, soft and pleasurable to wear. And you call it beloved, favored T-shirt.

Purchased a dozen years ago, Winner moved around its owner's bedroom. Sometimes it laid with other T-shirts in a storage box under the bed. Other times it got folded and stored in a dresser drawer. But its favorite place was on a hanger in the owner's closet.

Winner worked hard to comfort its owner. At first, it wanted to simply look good on the owner's body. It fit well, not too tight and not too loose. The medium gray cotton fabric went perfectly with the jeans the owner favored.

But Winner aged to the point of a tragic need to move on to T-shirt heaven. One side drooped and could not be reshaped. Part of the hem came unraveled and frayed. A sleeve developed a small split in a seam until the tear became an unrepairable hole.

It is with great heartache that Winner will at last be placed in the trash to go elsewhere. The owner can't face turning Winner into a dust rag.

Although the owner's heart aches over the loss, it is time to let Winner, beloved T-shirt go.

Be in peace, aged friend. You will long be remembered.

## TO TOWN AT CHRISTMASTIME

Bonnie Lacey Krenning

Being born in a back-woods community in rural Missouri, we were very isolated. At five years of age, in 1936, I had never been to town. One reason was we didn't have a car, only a team of horses and a wagon. Only rarely did any family have a car and town was about ten miles away.

At five years of age, I went to our one-room country school with my five older brothers. As Christmastime drew near, I heard that the small town was giving a bag of candy and an orange—I didn't know what an orange was—on Saturday before Christmas to all the grade school students in the district, if we came to town. Also, they said the movie picture show man was giving a free ticket to see the movie "Heidi" with Shirley Temple. I had never seen a movie picture.

So, on that Saturday morning before Christmas, Daddy and the boys hurried to do the chores, while Mom cooked breakfast and made a big box of peanut butter sandwiches for lunch. Mom said the food in town costs too much. I had heard before that when something costs too much, I couldn't have it.

We ate an early breakfast, then Daddy and the boys harnessed the team of horses up to the wagon. Our family of nine kids and Mom and Daddy climbed into the wagon. It was cold, so we sat in the wagon bed on heavy quilts and covered with more quilts, wearing heaving coats, stocking caps and billed caps for the older boys. Mom and Daddy climbed up on the spring seat in front, with Mom holding my baby brother, a toddler, also wrapped up in warm blankets.

Even though it was cold, with a blanket of snow on the ground we were too excited to care. The horses, also, were spirited and ready to go. We drove down the hill, across the homemade wooden bridge and up the next steep hill to the main road, about a quarter-mile from our house. We turned onto the gravel road and headed to town.

The cedar trees had snow piled high. It was so pretty. Then, after about an hour, Daddy turned onto the highway that ran by town. The highway looked so different. The boys said it was concrete; I had never seen concrete.

Daddy then turned onto the street to go downtown and we ran over some big, shiny rods lying across the street. I was scared because they were so bumpy under the metal wagon wheels. The boys said they were supposed to be there; they were train tracks. I had never head of trains, so I asked, "What are trains?" They said they were big engines that pulled boxcars. I still didn't understand!

Now we were on a brick street and there were shiny cars passing us. And there were such beautiful houses like I had never seen before. They were brick, stone and they painted some white, yellow and blue. They decorated them with bright lights, and wreaths with Santa Clauses and snowmen in the yards.

Then I looked ahead and saw a wonderland of bright colorful lights and decorations along the streets and storefronts everywhere. Mom said they were 'lectric lights. It was the first time I saw electric lights.

Daddy tied the team up and we jumped out, smiling and laughing, so excited. We hurried to the Community Building to get in line for our treats. As we waited in line, I could hear music, but I saw no one playing guitars or fiddles or singing. Mom said it was a record. I had never heard of a record.

We got our sack of candy and an orange, then the whole family walked on the sidewalks. The boys said the walks were concrete. I had never seen sidewalks before.

Soon we saw Santa coming toward us. I think he noticed our large family. Daddy was carrying my three-year-old brother. Since Santa was eye-to-eye with him, he paid special attention to my little brother, talking and laughing with him. When Santa walked on, my little brother said, "Daddy, 'dats not whiskers, 'dats jes' totten on his face!" Beards were common in the rural community and he knew the difference between cotton and real hair.

We all headed for the Ben Franklin Store, or as some called it "The Five and Dime Store." As we stepped inside, I couldn't believe my eyes: It seemed there were electric lights, garlands, ornaments, silver icicles, and angels everywhere. I had heard of angels; now I knew what they looked like.

The boys headed for boy's toys and Mom and I headed for girl's toys. There were teddy bears, play dishes, doll furniture and dolls. I headed for the baby dolls piled on a big tabletop. Some were big, and some were small. I picked up several and held them in my arms to check how they fit. Then I saw one tiny doll in just a diaper. I picked her up and held her; just the right fit and softness. Her skin was brown. I had never seen a brown doll before. Mom said it was a Negro doll and that some people have brown skin. I didn't know that!

I looked at the tag and it read 59 cents. I asked Mom if I could have it. She said we would have to ask Daddy. He came over and looked at the tag. He said it cost too much. I knew not to make a fuss if he said it cost too much, so I laid it back down.

We went out to the wagon and stood around eating our sandwiches. We went to the natural spring and drank water from a tin cup Mom brought for us.

Then Mom said it was one o'clock, time to go to the picture show. Daddy said to hurry back after the picture show, so we could get home to do the chores.

The movie house was crowded and noisy with all the school kids. As I tried to watch and hear, I couldn't understand how I could see the people in the picture and they were not there. And it really upset me that the woman who was so mean to Heidi.

When the movie was over, we hurried to the wagon. Daddy had fed the horses at noon, but they were ready to move on. So, we climbed back in the wagon to head for home, so Daddy and the boys could do the chores: feed the horses, cows, pigs and chickens, and milk the cows. Then Mom would have a good, hot supper ready. By that time, we would be starving after just having sandwiches for lunch.

A few days later, on Christmas morning, we woke up early to see what Santa Claus had put in our stockings. I checked my stocking, but did not notice what anyone else got, because the Negro baby doll was in my stocking.

An older brother had already told me that Daddy was Santa: That made the doll even more special.!

## MY WICHITA
### Don Boldea

What a magnificent sunrise.

On the coldest day, it'll warm your heart.

For that, no Wichitan will apologize.


As the morning begins, business is already a bustle.

Everyone is on the go.

Now is not the time to play, but rather to hustle.


It's the noon hour with the sun overhead.

There are still things to be done.

"Let's get busy" one Wichitan was to have said.


Afternoon matters need be attended.

Our community works hard.

Pride is real, so is honesty, neither is pretended.


The sun, the wonderful sun, is about to set.

Time to close from business and head for home.

Wichitans gather around their families, there is no reason to forget.

Our Lord is our salvation.

For us, his Son He did begat.


Wichitans give thanks in sweet anticipation.


Why this love, dedication and pride

to God, country and community?

Wichitans know His promise is true and tried!

## I SAW A HAWK IN THE MORNING SKY

Martha Williams Prentice

I saw a hawk

in the morning sky,

wings spread wide

and gliding high

above the treetops

in silence there.

I stopped,

and watched

her ride

the air.

## MAMA'S KITCHEN

### Rochelle Boster

After walking one quarter mile from the bus stop, I opened the door and the most wonderful smell of supper wrapped me in a magic "glad you're home" cloak! A hot cast-iron skillet on the GE Range held frying chicken that sputtered and popped, while its garlicky aroma permeated every corner of the kitchen.

A kitchen cabinet with an oak wood top stood on the wall right next to the wood stove. The happy part of that cabinet was a pull-out white enamel workspace where Mama kneaded bread and biscuits to my delight. I especially liked biscuits! Her hands were strong and with each kneading motion there was a rhythmic thump. I knew we were closer to the end product.

The excitement grew as she brought the rolling pin from the drawer. After flouring the surface of the workspace and the front of her dress, she rolled out the biscuit dough to just the right diameter. Mama used a yellowish-green aluminum glass with sharp edges to cut the biscuits into perfect round circles at least 1/2" high. Then she would pick up and place the biscuits on the baking sheet, spaced just right, so they didn't bump into one another.

She collected all the bits and pieces left, except two and molded the collection into a bonus biscuit with her hands. I was standing close because I knew that one of those bits was for me. When she gave it to me, I took it without hesitation and ate that biscuit dough with great appreciation. The smushy texture of the dough combined with the metallic taste of the baking powder, and just the right amount of salt was my heaven on earth.

Biscuits sat on the kitchen cabinet workspace waiting to feel the heat in the oven when the chicken was golden brown and crispy.

The wood stove close to the kitchen cabinet glowed red through its cast iron body. A very hot, well laid fire burned to make the kitchen a warm haven from the winter onslaught. Occasionally, baby Jersey calves shunned by their mothers were welcomed into the kitchen. They laid shivering on gunny sack beds at the base of the wood stove. Mama toweled them dry and heated bottles of milk to warm their stomachs.

My favorite room in the house was my mama's kitchen. With mama there, the best place in the world.

How do you describe a place with more purposes than the obvious one? Mama's kitchen was figuratively the center of the house.

Our family was large by some standards, six kids and Mama and Daddy. I had the last position with all the perks you might imagine. The next oldest child was ten years older than me. And the age span grew to 17 years. The older kids were fast approaching independence by the time I came along. So, my advantage was, I had a one-to-one access and attention from my parents.

The kitchen grew into the center for sibling walk-ins for meals. Life's challenges became topics at the kitchen table. We strategized college careers and explored financing for them. We introduced significant others to the family. And we talked about wedding bells on the horizon.

When it was just the three of us that kitchen afforded the opportunity to discuss much more. We talked about my folks' financial status. And we discussed religious enigmas, the Korean Conflict where my oldest brother was, and politics. It was an open forum. They gave me equal status. I learned to debate, develop a large atypical vocabulary for my age, and to argue with respect.

As the years went by the kitchen changed with trending fashion. The GE Range remained the same, but they traded the wooden table for a gray Formica table with matching gray padded chairs. The wood stove gave way to convenience with a propane fueled stove that didn't require cutting wood or gathering kindling. But the saddest of all, the kitchen cabinet ended up on the junk pile in favor of white metal cabinets, uppers and lowers.

The updating didn't change the real importance of the kitchen! Mama still fixed great meals that satisfied the stomach while the conversation satisfied the soul. They welcomed everyone, including neighbors, friends, and family and had a place set for them at the table. Mama's kitchen was not only the center of the house it was the heart of the family.

Excerpt from Mulberry Hill Farm Memories, R. Boster

## MEDICINE MAN

Bonnie Creekmore

Dear little Joshua—
Medicine man
Helping Grandma
Get well if he can.
Bright dandelions
All butter yellow
Held in the fist
Of this sweet little fellow
Offered in love
To a Grandma quite ill—
'Tis a potion far stronger
Than a pharmacy pill.
First he charmed,
Then sacrificed.
The offering was
The final price.
The medicine man,
His work now done,
Goes home to be
My daughter's son.

# MY CHRISTMAS TREES

Bonnie Lacey Krenning

When I was five years old, I saw my first Christmas tree in my one-room country school in Cedar County Missouri. In that community, usually only schools and churches had Christmas trees. And there were no churches close enough for us to attend by team and wagon.

I thought the tree was beautiful so when I got home I asked Daddy if we could have a Christmas tree. The next day he took me with him out to the pasture and cut a tree for me and my brothers. There were no electric lights, but my brothers and I made decorations and hung them. In my mind now, it was the most beautiful of all our Christmas trees over the decades.

Eventually I grew up, sorta. Bill and I married in May after I finished high school. He worked for the Missouri State Highway Department with a group of men painting bridges. He was the only married man, besides the boss. The job usually entailed moving every two to four weeks throughout the middle and west side of the state. The men, except the boss, stayed in hotels.

So, just before we married Bill bought a used travel-trailer; a camper. He was the only man on the crew that owned a camper besides the boss.

I thought it was a castle: Beautiful plywood paneling, a domed ceiling and kitchen build-ins. The front room measured seven by nine feet with a sofa and a desk in that. It was plenty of space for us. I'm giving you these dimensions for a reason.

In August we moved from Kansas City to Boonville, Missouri to paint a large bridge over the Missouri River and we stayed there until after Christmas.

I settled into my dream world of being a housewife. I ordered many household items from the Sears Roebuck catalog; and some clothing. Then, in early November I received a Christmas catalog from the Roebucker, as we called it and I started looking, dreaming and even planning on a Christmas tree and ordering decorations.

Then Bill's family invited us to their home, which was about an hour's drive away from where we lived for Thanksgiving Dinner. They lived in the country and had Cedar trees, considered a nuisance, growing in the pasture. I asked Bill if we could get a Christmas tree while we were there. He looked at me quizzically, his dimples deepening, and said, "Where will we put it?" Then he said, "Oh, I guess so."

After Thanksgiving Dinner Bill and his Dad went out in the pasture and cut a six-food Cedar tree and loaded it into the trunk of our '37 Chevy coupe. When we got home, Bill made a stand and fastened the tree to it. It nearly touched the ceiling and, since it was a bushy Cedar, it spread out over four feet and filled two-thirds of the double doorway. We had to slide it in sideways.

Unknown to Bill, but because he had told me, he would get the tree, I had ordered Christmas decorations and stored them in my closet. He put the lights up for me; the first time I had tree lights, and I finished the decorating. He didn't show his excitement like I did, but he made sure all the other men including the boss and his wife came over to see the tree.

Our first tree, and the ritual has continued, since I was five years old, over the decades, with a live tree. I sometimes thought we should have taken pictures of our first Christmas tree; Bill and mine. He had a camera. But, maybe what I remember is better than the black and white pictures would show.

## THE TOY

Coe Holden

Your favorite Toy will always be there for you

When you are blue, it is there for you.

When you are sick, it is waiting for you.

It may be a little faded and need some repair, but it will be faithful forever.

Through the years when you out grow it, it gets put in a box for a long time.

And some day, when you have a boy or girl of your own, it can be a favorite Toy again.

## SOMETIMES I SEE A SIMPLE THING

Martha Williams Prentice

Sometimes I see a simple thing…

a curling petal, an insect wing

a fallen leaf, a drying pod

shriveled bark, yellowed sod.

I take a moment to give it thought…

and tears well up from in my heart

to fill my eyes to overflow

and stream my face in silence slow.

## CONUNDRUM

### Rochelle Boster

Searching for me,

Lost to myself?

Searching for love,

Is it true or false?

Searching for identity,

Confused with what others want?

Searching for security,

When and what will I eat?

Searching for my livelihood,

Day to day job or my passion?

Searching for friendship,

Trust others to like me for me?

Discovery,

I love deeply, but hurt more!

Discovery,

I am strong, but need assurance!

Discovery,

I am intelligent, but need affirmation!

Discovery,

I am stubborn, but need to humble myself and ask for help!

Discovery,

I need to ask more questions, but listen to the answers!

Teach me, talk to me, trust me

Believe in Me!

# WHITE CHRISTMAS

Bonnie Lacey Krenning

About a month before Christmas in 1941, when I was ten years old, my family moved from my childhood farm in Cedar County, Missouri, so we could all be closer to Daddy. He worked as a carpenter on building a military base near Joplin, Missouri. World War II had not yet started, but there were signs on the horizon.

A few days before we left the farm, our old speckled rooster woke me. I looked out the bedroom window. The sun was just coming up and a new heavy blanket of snow had fallen in the night.

Snow covered the ground and piled high on the cedar trees and the bare limbs of the birch, sycamore, hickory and walnut trees. The sun shone on the glistening icicles hanging from the eves and the snow. It was more beautiful than the electric lights I saw in town a few years ago.

Daddy was home. He had been working away from home on defense work for several months and was not home often. He didn't have a car. My brothers were big enough to run the farm. The folks decided to sell the farm and move close to where he worked. They auctioned the animals and equipment, and they sold the farm.

Daddy then bought a used car and borrowed a truck to haul the furniture. With the boys helping we loaded up and headed for Joplin and our new home. As we drove into Joplin, it was night time and Christmas lights seemed to surround us; a wonderland.

We arrived at a big stone house that Daddy had rented in the country. And we had electricity for the first time. But the bad odor of the coal-burning stove was awful! On the farm we burned wood, sometimes cedar, and it always smelled good. There was, however, a radio. I had never seen or heard one. Now I could listen to music all the time.

Never mind we still had an outhouse and a well.

As the family listened to church music on the radio on Sunday morning, December 6, 1941, the news man interrupted the program to say someone had bombed Pearl Harbor.

Instantly everything changed for the family and for the country. I had one brother in the navy, another a Medic in the army and three more married brothers eligible for the draft. I had never seen my folks more anxious and depressed. Mom was tearful much of the time and I had nightmares and sleep-walked. These were the brothers that had carried me to school and looked out for me: they might die like the men at Pearl Harbor.

I had just started to our new school. It was crowded but nice. I didn't understand how it got heated, there were no stoves. There were four rooms, eight grades and over one-hundred students; about twenty-five students in each room. I soon missed my friends in the one-room school back home, with a heating stove, where I knew everyone, and everyone knew me. I had the same teacher for over five years. At the new school I knew no one except my four brothers and didn't see them often.

The other kids were mostly "city kids" and thought we talked funny; hillbillies that we were. Their clothes were different, too; "store-bought." My brothers wore overalls, but Mom made my dresses from printed feed sacks on the treadle sewing machine. I thought they were "purdy." I noticed that in the bathrooms—I didn't know about bathrooms—that the other girls wore "store-bought" panties. They noticed that I wore flannel bloomers that Mom and I made. I was used to my friends back home liking my clothes; their clothes were about the same as mine.

The teacher in my crowded fifth and sixth-grade classroom was nice to me. As we were practicing for the Christmas program, she noticed that I knew the songs, which I learned from the radio and was singing out, even though I was so shy I would hardly talk. She asked me to sing a solo, "Up on the Housetop" in the program; and I did!

Due to my teacher back home, my big brothers and Daddy teaching me math, I was ahead of most of the kids in my class in division and multiplication. The teacher had me help her work with the other kids. That helped some to make me become more accepted.

We had art classes which I loved and had never had before. But I was always drawing and coloring. Being told that all colors came from red, yellow and blue was a revelation to me. I had to check it out before believing it. After much experimenting; yes, it was so!

There was a kitchen, and the cooks prepared hot lunches; another first for me. No more peanut butter and honey sandwiches. The cooks soon called me their "good eater." I wonder why?

One evening just before Christmas, I was listening to the radio and heard the beautiful song, "White Christmas." Bing Crosby was singing, "I'm dreaming of a white Christmas, just like the ones I used to know, where the tree tops glisten...." Leaning back in the wooden rocking chair, I closed my eyes and saw myself back on the farm, looking out the window at that beautiful snow scene. I wanted to go back to the farm for Christmas and be with my school friends and sing with them.

We moved three more times during the war as Daddy felt he needed to do his part in helping to build military bases and defense plants. The best part was they drafted two other brothers, and the four brothers were in combat on the front lines for three or four years. They all came back safely. Only one suffered a minor injury after the war.

Even now, I never hear the song "White Christmas" without going back to the beautiful scene etched in my memory from my childhood of that morning on the farm so many decades ago. There has never been a picture, photograph or moving picture that can match the memory of that scene.

## A DRAGONFLY FROM NEARBY GLADE
### Martha Williams Prentice

A dragonfly from nearby glade
suddenly lit upon a blade
  in the flower vase of clear cut-glass,
  upon a base of footed brass,
    placed on a table small and round
    with lilac lace draped to the ground
      positioned out by sycamore tree
      where I have my morning tea.

The shear double wings on blue and green
in morning sunlight glistening sheen
  are open and held in proud display
  for my delight this special day,
    to be remembered with a smile
    these private moments shared awhile.
      With pen in hand in days to come
      I'll think of him and write a poem.

## THE CHRISTMAS CABIN

Ann Alvis

Rushing down the top stairs, Marie almost tripped over the last step trying to gather everything up she needed for her trip. She was excited, for the long-awaited time at the Christmas Lodge. A Christmas get away at a resort she had won in a contest. A dream of hers for years.

"Mom, why don't you take the plane? It's faster and I would not worry about you on the road," Jessica, her daughter, said as she followed Marie to the kitchen.

"Nonsense, then I couldn't drop the food and other items I gathered off for the shelter on the way. Do you know they feed hundreds? I want to help this year," she said as she picked up the food bags and headed to the car. "You never know, Jessica, who might need this food." She looked up from the side of the car. "We all need to do our share. This time, I want to give a little. Being blessed all these years, I want to bless others."

"I know what you mean, Mom, but you have so much here. I'm sure they'll be okay. I worry about you." Jessica stood by the red Buick Lacrosse with her chin on top of the door.

"Nothing will happen. I feel good about this trip. I feel something magical just might develop."

"Mom, please! They're expecting a snow storm. I don't want you stranded."

"It's settled. I' will help with the food. Don't worry about the snow. I'll be there before it starts. You will not talk me out of it." She tapped her daughter on the shoulder and gave her a smile.

Jessica followed Marie back into the kitchen and helped her grab the few bags left on the counter. She glanced over her shoulder and smiled. "Mom, I want you to go. Since I can't convince you to fly, well, then drive carefully. And call when you get there."

Marie walked and hugged her daughter. "Honey, I'll be fine. You know how I love to drive and I will be careful."

In the garage again, she opened the car door, sat down, and looked at Jessica. "This will be a trip to remember." She waved as she pulled out of the garage.

As she drove down the road, she turned the radio on to Christmas music, keeping it low enough to hear her GPS. Yes, I feel this will be an awesome trip. Pleased, she sang "White Christmas" with Bing Crosby.

"Turn right," the GPS announced. "In four hundred feet, turn left." She did not pay much attention to the road as she drove, relying on the instructions given to her. She listened and sang to the Christmas carols playing on the radio.

Several hours had passed, and it began to snow along with a dense fog, making it hard to see. "Didn't expect this," she said as she turned her radio off to focus more on the road. "Wish I had gotten a hot cup of coffee at that last stop." She needed to stay awake until she reached a hotel.

Looking at the clock on the console, she realized she'd been on the road six and a half hours already. This was taking her longer than expected. She should have made it to the shelter by now.

"In one thousand feet, turn right," the voice from the GPS commanded.

The snow fell heavier, and the wind gained speed making it harder to see the road.

"Yes. Yes... if I can see the turn where is that road?" She propped herself close to the steering wheel trying to see if it would make it easier to get her bearings. She needed to find that turn off. The windshield wipers were going at full speed, pushing the snow off as fast as it came down.

"Did I miss it?" Marie asked in frustration. She needed to find a place to turn around. Stopping on the side of the road to catch a quick breath, she grumbled, "Okay, GPS, where to now?"

She tapped the GPS. "Really... now you want to stop?"

She picked up her phone from beside her on the passenger's seat. "No, you can't be dead too!" She hoped she'd packed the charger. Maybe she should have flown.

Frustrated, she started the car and pulled out to continue straight on the road. Surely it would lead her somewhere. She took deep breaths as it got harder to see. The wind was causing large snow drifts. Driving at a low speed, she wasn't sure if the roads might be slick from the temperature drop outside.

When she could make out a blinking light ahead, she sighed in relief. "Fi-Ply, something." But her hopes faded as she realized it was only a warning sign.

"You've got to be kidding me! I don't know where I'm at, no GPS. Lord, I need a little help here please." She laid her head on the steering wheel with tears in her eyes.

A few minutes passed, and she sat up straight. Lord, you're my pilot. Starting the car, she backed up and turned left, wiping away a few more tears.

After an hour, she realized she wasn't getting any closer to a town. Her stomach knotted. The snow was still falling and nothing in sight.

As she saw a large log in the road, she turned on a small road. Last thing I need is to get stuck or in a wreck. With each passing minute, Marie got more scared. Her gas was getting low, and she needed to stop and look for her charger to call for help. She searched for a spot to pull over.

The Buick slid on some ice. Trying to control the car, she came to a sudden stop as she hit something in the road. She saw she had just missed a truck that had slid off the road and was in a small ditch. "Really?" Straightening, she rubbed her head.

Looking up, she saw a man running toward her car. He wore a dark blue suit with a black trench coat. He had his hands crossed in front of him trying to stay warm. "Are you okay?" he asked.

"Yea, I think so. I hit my head, but I think I'm okay," Marie said as she rolled down her window. "What's going on?"

"The road is a sheet of ice and I landed here." He pointed to his gray Dodge Ram. "I thought the monster could handle it. Now I've got a broken axle, not going anywhere. And with the looks of your car you're not either." He stood shivering, holding his arms together.

"What do we do now? We're in the middle of nowhere. Do you have a cell phone?" Marie asked.

"I can't get any bars out here."

"Do you know where we are?"

"I have no idea. My GPS stopped, and I missed my turn. The bridge was out, and I ended up here in the middle of who knows where." He shivered more. "This one thing I know, the snow is falling faster, and it's getting colder. I spotted an old cabin a half mile up the hill. I think our best chances of survival is there."

Marie rolled her window almost closed and wiped tears away. She pushed her long blonde hair back with one hand. She had a giving heart and helped others when she could. Now she was relying on a stranger to help her.

"Lady, I promise I won't hurt you. But if you stay here, you'll freeze to death. This weather will only get worse."

She sat there for a moment staring at the man's dark hair that had gray mixed in with it. His eyes were a deep blue and she thought they had twinkled a little. Finally, she opened her door.

As she stepped out, he reached down to help her. When she almost fell, he caught her and helped her stand up.

She wrapped her coat tight around her. "Thank you. Is there someone at the cabin?"

"I'm not sure. Let me help you." He held Marie's arm as she stepped over the log she had ran into.

"Should have flown," she mumbled.

"You and me both. I had to see the country. The cabin is right up here." He pointed up the hill. "Oh, Raymond's the name."

"Marie," she said, holding tight to his arm. "We need to get my bag out of the trunk. It has my phone charger in it."

Raymond walked over and popped her trunk and lifted out a red bag. "I don't think we can get any service here, but a change of dry clothes after walking in the snow sounds good."

He went to grab his bag from the back of the truck. "You ready?" He held his elbow out to her.

The cabin seemed like miles away with the wind and snow blowing in their faces and the temperature falling fast. The snow had drifted in spots. Marie's high heels were not the best shoes to walk in the snow. She didn't complain, but she felt the cold rushing through her body and pulling her strength away. The snow got deeper and at times it came up to her knees. She struggled through the cold, trying to keep calm.

At last a rundown looking cabin came into sight. It had a large porch with broken railings around it and a few broken steps. It looked like no one had been there for years. Yet it was more inviting than the snow outside.

Raymond knocked on the door and looked over at Marie. "Hey, you never know." He smiled. When he realized the door was unlocked, he pushed it open and stepped inside. "Hello, is anyone here? Hello?"

He smiled at her and held the door open. "Seems no one is home."

"It's a little dark in here and smelly too," she said.

"Well. It will get darker soon. It looks like there might be a full moon which will help us see a little better."

"What next? My daughter worried I'd get stranded. And here I am out in the middle of nowhere." Marie wanted to sit down and cry but feared the frigid cold temperatures might freeze her tears. She wanted to be strong, let him know she could carry her weight in this bad situation.

"I need to see if there is some wood around here, so we can keep warm. Seems there are a few logs near the fireplace. It will keep the place warm for a couple hours. I hope there's more somewhere." Raymond stomped the snow off his shoes. "I'll be around close."

As he shut the door and walked around the cabin, Marie stood in the middle of the cabin. She looked at the cob webs in the corner and eyed mouse droppings on the floor, trying not to cry. She needed to keep calm to survive.

The moon gave enough light in the cabin that she could explore and see what she could find. "A wonderful weekend?" She snorted. Guess I won't forget this one if I survive.

Passing by a closed door she heard a loud banging coming from inside. Then another came as she put her ear up to the door. She screamed and jumped back, thinking an animal might be inside. "Oh my gosh! Oh my gosh!"

Raymond came running in, yelling, "What's wrong?"

"There's something in that room and its loud!" she cried. "It could be a bear, a tiger, a… whatever. I know that there is something banging around in that room!" She pointed at the door.

He laughed a little and started to open the door.

"Are you crazy?" She pulled back on his arm.

He touched her hand and looked at her. "It's okay. I promise you there is nothing in here."

As he opened the door, he said, "I found a rack of wood right outside the window. I need to throw it inside, so it will dry so we can burn it. There's a little dry wood near the fireplace, enough until the other wood dries in here. Wet wood doesn't burn good."

He turned away from the door that worried her, opened the window, and went toward the front door. "I'll be done soon, and I'll start us a fire. You want to check and see what other goods this cabin has to offer?" He winked at her.

"Now... if I don't feel like a fool." Marie watched Raymond go back outside. She walked around the small cabin. Opening another door, she discovered a large closet. She stood in front of it and her eyes filled with tears.

Raymond had just finished throwing the last of the fire wood through the window, when he saw a light come on inside. He opened the door and looked over at Marie.

"I found these blankets, lamps that run on batteries and lots of batteries. And even a small radio." She held them up as excited as if they were a Christmas gift. Picking up a piece of paper, she added, "I also found this note."

She read: I am the owner of this cabin. If you find yourself stranded here, help yourself. Hopefully someone will find you soon.

"Well, God has watched over us. Though there isn't any gas in the generator, the lamps will come in handy and we still need some food," Raymond said as he opened the cabinets.

"He probably didn't have time to stock it full for us," she said, giggling a little. "But if you're up to it, we can go back to my car. I have five sacks of food and a few other items in a box that might come in handy."

"You must have been going to the shelter off Highway forty."

"Yes, I was, and you?"

"Won a trip to the Christmas Lodge and thought I'd enjoy the beautiful country and had plans to drop off a few things too. Well, we need to get going, not much light left. And the snow doesn't look like it's ending, could be over a foot soon."

Walking back to the car was harder this time. It was colder, and the snow was deeper. Marie had found a pair of boots in the closet. Even though they were three sizes too big, they were better than walking in high heels in the snow.

Limbs from some trees had already been weighed down and you could hear the crackling as if they were getting ready to break. They heard owls in the trees. Several deer ran across the field ahead and a small deer fawn trailed behind. The sight made Marie smile.

"Cold, but pretty," she said as she glanced around.

Finally reaching the car, Marie took a few bags. But Raymond insisted on carrying the box and most of the bags.

Now that the wind was blowing in colder air she shivered more. She kept trudging her way through the snow. When she looked up at Raymond, she shook her head and smiled. "You look like Santa with a box, minus the red suit." She snickered.

He laughed as they made their way back to the cabin. As they approached the door, he kicked it open. They hurried to place the food on the dusty counter. After Marie turned the lamp on, she went through the boxes. She took things out and laid them on the counter.

Raymond went to the fireplace, grabbed a shovel, and removed the ashes. "I'll get this started and you can have the honor of seeing what we have to eat."

She turned and glanced out the window. "Looks like we're moving in." The sun was almost down, and the bright full moon made the smooth snow glitter. 'It's beautiful, the moonlight on the snow. The snowflakes seem to sparkle."

Raymond turned and must have seen the worry on her face. "Hey, we have heat, food."

"And coffee!" Marie added in a grateful voice. "And I found a coffee pot."

"That sounds like a winner." When he looked toward her, he smiled. "It's an old camping one, which we can put over the fire." He stood and walked to the back room, then carried logs in and started a fire. "That coffee sure will taste good, even the smell warms me inside."

She poured him a cup of coffee and sat near the fire to sip her coffee. "How long do you think we'll be here?"

"I'm not sure. It depends on the snow, how long it will last." Sitting beside her, he reached over to touch her hand. "When we don't show back home after the weekend, I'm sure they will start looking."

"Were in the middle of nowhere," she reminded him, sounding anxious.

"Yea, but I can almost guess whoever left this stuff will check the cabin out after the snow stops and they can get through."

"You really think so?"

He nodded, smiling. "I always say, keep positive and pray." He paused. "We must get another necessary chore done before we turn in for the night."

"What's that?" Marie took another sip of coffee and looked up as he stood.

"Buckets of snow."

What? Snow in a bucket?" she questioned him.

"We need buckets of snow to melt, so when we can use the bathroom. Without the generator having gas we have no electricity to run water to the sink or bathroom," he explained. "We'll use the melted snow to flush the toilet. That's probably the bad smell in here, but I'll take care of it. We can also use the melted water to drink and wash with. I saw several buckets outside, just wanted to warm up first."

He walked over and grabbed the large coat hanging on the back of the front door. She stood and dropped the blanket she'd tucked around her. "I can help."

"That's okay. You have a cut on your head that's still bleeding. And you're still cold. You need to take it easy," Raymond said in concern.

"I'm okay, let me help. You don't have to do all this by yourself. I'm capable of helping you."

"Okay, get your coat. Let's get this over with."

Marie grabbed her heavy coat off a hook on the back of the kitchen door. They walked outside, and the snow blew so hard, it hurt as it came across their faces.

She struggled to shovel the snow into the buckets. Her body hurt, and she couldn't stop shaking. But she kept shoveling. She didn't want him to think she was helpless.

Raymond studied her, and Marie knew he saw that she was having a hard time. Looking worried, he said, "I think we have enough."

He walked over and grabbed the buckets. "You go inside. Get warm, maybe check on the coffee."

Marie turned and slowly walked inside, holding onto the walls trying not to fall. She shivered, her body felt frozen. She went over to the fireplace and flopped down, grabbed her blanket and continued shivering. She closed her eyes as she tried to catch her breath and shook uncontrollably. Soon she laid on the floor, shivering more. Her body went still as she passed out.

Raymond walked in with the buckets and saw Marie struggling. He feared that she had gotten too cold and her body was shutting down. He rushed over to her and felt her body. It was ice cold and he could not get a response from her.

He put more logs on the fire and found more blankets. "Sorry, sweetheart, think nothing of this." He carefully removed her blouse, then pulled his shirt off and crawled under the covers, bringing her close to him. It was the only way he knew to keep her alive. He needed to bring up her body heat slowly, so her heart would not stop.

"Please, Lord, take care of her," he prayed.

Marie woke up a few hours later and found Raymond asleep next to her. Startled, she pushed him and asked, "What are you doing?"

"Keeping you alive," he answered groggily. "I think you have a concussion and the cold brought your body temp down. You were freezing." He looked uncomfortable but determined. "This was the only way I knew to warm you without your heart giving out. Trust me, I'm a gentleman. I just didn't want to see anything happen to you."

Marie laid there and studied his eyes and knew he was telling the truth. She felt so much warmer and didn't want to move. She appreciated his compassion. "Thank you."

"Maybe some breakfast will make you feel better." He pushed the covers off and slipped bis shirt back on. "I'll leave the room, so you can have some privacy. Then I'll be back to fix us something to eat."

She sat up and waited till she wasn't dizzy. Grabbing her red bag close to her, she pulled out the Christmas sweater she had packed and slipped it over her head.

Raymond returned and came over to help her off the floor. "Here, sit in the chair and I'll fix some coffee. It'll warm you up." He wrapped a blanket around her.

"Who are you?"

"I'm Raymond." He looked at her in concern.

"Are you sure you're not an angel, sent here to watch over me," she whispered.

"You know anyone can be one of the Lord's Angels, if he chooses. You never know. But I think I'm just Raymond for now, stuck in the same snow storm as you are."

Marie rose and walked over to the table. "I'll have a cup of coffee with my angel."

They were silent as he made them something to eat. Finally, he handed her a plate with some fried potatoes. "We can have these for our breakfast."

"Tell me, Raymond, what is it that you do?" Marie asked as she brought the hot coffee to her nose to smell the sweet aroma.

"I do a bit of everything."

She stood, thinking about what he'd said, and walked over to the window. The blanket still wrapped around her kept her warm as she looked out at the snow. "This getaway was supposed to be a chance maybe for my life to turn around. It's funny that they say come to the Christmas Lodge to maybe find love."

Still gazing out the window, she sipped her coffee. She laughed. "A woman my age thinking of such fairy tales. The snow is so pretty and white, smooth without footsteps. The trees with icicles hanging from the limbs. It's a winter wonderland."

She returned to the fireplace and sit down to stare into the flames. "It was a nice dream, the Christmas Lodge."

"It's okay to dream," Raymond said, sounding thoughtful.

Lost in her own thoughts, she said, "Now, I'm here in a cabin, in a snow storm. For who knows how long."

"You need to be positive about this," he attempted to lighten the moment. "Hey, when the snow stops we can go sledding, have snowball fights, make some snow ice cream. If you feel like it."

Marie turned and found him smiling at her with his kind face. "You make it sound fun being stranded here."

"Life is what we make it, in good or bad satiations." Raymond said as he lifted his coffee cup toward her. "It's almost Christmas. Well, the snow outside makes it feel like that. But I am thankful the Lord has taken care of us. We could be popsicles out there. I always had a soft spot in my heart for Christmas."

Raymond lifted his gaze to Marie. Wondering why out of all the places and people to get stranded with, he was here with her. He saw her warm but lonely heart. He wanted to show her life is good in any situation, and he knew then what he wanted to do. Standing up from the table, he grabbed his coat from the wall peg.

"Where are you going?" Marie asked, appearing puzzled.

"I have to get something. I won't be long." He opened the door and pushed it closed to keep the snow and the cold wind from rushing in.

Marie shook her head. "Wonder what he forgot?"

A short time later, Marie heard Raymond yell at her to open the door. She hurried over, pulled the handle, and the door swung open by the force of the wind.

He stood in the doorway, seeing her surprised look, and grinned.

"A tree! You got a tree? Are you crazy? It's cold. You could have frozen," she chided, smiling.

"Oh, this isn't any tree." He strode inside and leaned it in the corner by the fireplace. "This is a very lonely tree, that wants to be our Christmas tree." He pulled some pine cones from his pocket. "And here are a few decorations we can use to make her pretty. She's not much, but she'll do. What do you think?" he asked, sounding wary.

Marie walked over to the tree and touched the branches. She looked up at Raymond with tears in her eyes. "You got this tree for Christmas?"

"What is Christmas without a tree?" He smiled at her. "What do you think?" he asked again.

"She's beautiful." As she looked at the tree, she felt humbled. "Thank you. Now it really feels like Christmas."

"Well, let's get her in a bucket and see what we can do with her." He lifted the tree and placed it in a bucket Marie quickly brought to him.

She walked in excitement over to her purse and pulled out a small bag. "I have a sewing kit with needles and thread. There's popcorn in one of those bags we carried in earlier. We can string it for the tree."

He grinned. "Great idea! She'll be the prettiest tree ever."

They worked together to string popcorn and placed it on the tree with the pine cones. Then Raymond handed Marie a wood star he had put together with twigs. "The finishing touches."

As she placed it on top of the tree, she turned and headed toward another box they'd brought inside. "Wait one more thing!" She took out several little candles that had batteries. She placed one under the star and a few on the tree limbs. They turned each on and saw the glow.

Marie walked backwards until Raymond stopped her. 'It's beautiful," she whispered.

"That it is." He looked at the tree, then over to her. "Very beautiful."

They turned the radio on, found some Christmas music, and sat by the fire. They sang along with many of the songs, laughing and smiling at each other.

Later, she slipped under the covers and watched the warm flame in the fireplace until she closed her eyes.

Marie woke up to the smell of coffee. Raymond sat at the table dozing off. "Merry Christmas!" she called out, startling him.

She got up, walked to the table, and sat down.

Raymond reached down by the side of his chair and brought up a bag. He handed it to her. "Merry Christmas."

Surprised, she opened the bag and pulled out a miniature cabin made from twigs. She lifted it up and stared at it. "This is the cabin we're at. Did you make this?"

He nodded. "I wanted to give you something to remember that this Christmas wasn't all that bad."

"It's beautiful. Thank you. This is a good Christmas." She smiled at him, then stood and touched his shoulder, giving him a small kiss on his cheek. "I'll never forget this Christmas."

******

In the days that followed, the snow stopped, and the sun came out. Marie and Raymond had snowball fights which he always let her win. Sometimes she fell in the snow and when he tried to help her up, she'd pull him down. Both would laugh. They found old trash can lids and he pushed her around and they would laugh so hard they'd fall over in the snow.

"I think some warm coffee is in order," she said and picked herself up from the snow.

He laughed. 'Think you may be right."

Inside the cabin again, Marie sipped her coffee, looking over at Raymond." I never dreamed I could have such a good time stranded."

"It has been fun and the company's good too." He stood up and glanced out the window, appearing thoughtful.

Early the next day the sun came out, and both again headed out in the snow.

"Hey! Raymond, look at the snowman I built. It looks just like you," she teased.

Raymond laughed at seeing the snowman had six arms. "Very funny."

He chased her around the snowman until they fell beside each other. He looked into her eyes and before she knew it he leaned over and kissed her. When he leaned away, he asked, "Can your snowman do that?"

Marie smiled at him, uncertain. "I think we need to go in, I need a cup of coffee."

"So do I." He held out his hand to help her up. As he pulled her close to him, he looked ready to kiss her again. Instead he reached down and picked her scarf up and handed it to her.

******

A few more days went by still stuck at the cabin. They became closer. Marie regretted the day someone knocked on the door.

When she opened the door, she found a tall, heavy man standing on the porch. "There's a few people gone missing. Seen your cars down the road. Thought you might be up here."

As she stepped aside, he walked in and looked around. "My name's Levi and this here is my cabin. Funny thing right before the storm hit, something told me to get this cabin ready for some folks visiting. Well, got most of the stuff. I see you took care of more things." Glancing at the coffee, picking up a cup. "You mind?"

"No, go right ahead, and thank you!" Marie said to Levi.

"Got my truck and some guys coming and towing your cars into town. I figured with the snow storm moving in so fast, this here place would have her some company. Seems every snow storm that finds its way around here at Christmastime brings in someone. That's why I gave it a name. This here is the Christmas Cabin. I'm glad you folks found it. How long you been here?" he asked as he sipped his coffee.

"About six days," Raymond told him. "I'm grateful for the cabin and the supplies you left here."

"It isn't nothing, just trying to help folks that might need it. Good thing you all had your own food, or you might have had to go hunting for some." The old gentlemen laughed.

"Just how far is the next town?" Raymond asked.

"About forty, forty-five miles. You got stranded in the right place or you probably wouldn't have made it."

Marie' and Raymond gathered their things and loaded them in the truck, Marie took one last look at the cabin, then at Raymond. "It's funny, I think I will miss this old cabin."

"Me too, but I'll miss the company more."

As they drove away, neither of them had much to say on the way into town. They just knew the long, cold snowy days were over and they would return to their lives once again.

Raymond helped Marie out of the truck. "I'd like to see you again."

"I'd like that too." She looked at him and smiled.

He reached over and kissed her. "Thank goodness for the Christmas Cabin."

She smiled again. "To the Christmas Cabin."